Sunshine Through Darkness

Tonetta Chester

Sunshine Through Darkness

Published by: TC Publishing Group
2870 Peachtree Road Suite# 616
Atlanta, GA 30305
 www.tcpublishinggroup.com

International Standard Book Number: 9781935714026
Library of Congress Control Number: 2010904387

This book is a work of fiction. All names, characters, places, and incidents are purely fictional. Any resemblance to any actual events, locales, or persons, living or dead, actual events, establishments, organizations, and locales are intended to give the fiction a sense of reality and authenticity and are coincidental. Other names, characters, places, events, and incidents are either products of the author's imagination or are used fictitiously.

Cover by: Extreme Media

www.tonettachester.com

In loving memory of

Jerriff Omar Harper

October 29, 1981–October 30, 2006

I love you!

Chuck, it's only been four years but it seems like **forever**…..

Don't forget to tell the people that you love "I love you" every chance you get, because you never know when you will see or speak to them for the last time.

Love always and forever.

Contents

Green Eyes preview

Acknowledgments

Thank you, Lord, for every experience that you bring me on this journey called life. I have overcome so many things with you. I love you, Lord. Special thanks to my daughter, Skylar Ariza, my goddaughter, Raymondra Saffold; my parents, Elaine and Samuel Jones; my birth father, Tony Chester; my brothers, Tony Chester and Samuel Jones; my sisters, Timakii Chester and Ay Jones; my special aunt , Gazette Burke; my special cousins Missy Bailey, Lil Warren Freeman.

When I look back over the years, a few people stand out: Yolanda, Nancy, Krahima, Ronald, Kevin, Dwayne, St. Clair, Corey, Demon, Nikki, and Damien aka Grave Bigger. Thank you for being my friends—I love you all!

I would also like to thank *you,* the person reading this, because you took the time to buy my second book. Thank you for your support; it means so much to me. Special thanks to everyone at TC Publishing Group and TC & Associates. We did it again! I don't know what I would have done without you all. I am so blessed to have a crew full of wonderful people. You guys are the best! Thanks!

Ilda Dania Njango, thank you for pushing me to do more, for challenging everything. Girl, you make it hard for me some nights but I love you for that.

Kole Black, thank you, you have been a true teacher! I have learned so much from you. You've inspired me in so many ways.

The late night pep talks and writing kept me focused. I can't wait to work on a project with you.

Victor G, thanks for always being available to listen. You're the best! Love ya

Kejuan B, through our ups and downs we have always manage to be friends. Love ya KB.

RonDre K, who would have known? It's been seven years— seven years! Dre, you have always reminded me of my uncle, but you're more like my big brother! I can call you for anything; you always listen and give some of the best advice.

Kyaysha W (Kya-Kya), you're always a phone call or a flight away. I cherish our friendship, I love you like family. We share some wonderful memories and some painful ones too, but no matter what, we've stood strong through many things.

Tica R, wow, we have come so far. I remember when I didn't like you! Those two had us fooled! (Smile) *Chuck and Raha,* now we talk every day. How crazy is that? Thanks for calling me on that so very painful day, October 30, 2006. You opened the door to a wonderful friendship; I can truly call you an angel. It's been a blessing to have you as a friend. Love ya girl!

Gary S, thanks for your support and always keeping your word!

Orlando G, no matter what, you always come through. I don't know what I would do without you sometimes. Everyone needs a friend like you. Love ya.

Brandon L, thanks for always been honest. Friends for life! I love you BL.

Dorsel B, boy, boy, boy! I'll never forget the first day we met — you had me in tears. You're an angel and I'm blessed to have met you. I mean that from the bottom of my heart! I love you (finish that project baby).

Tony S, thanks for your understanding. I know you, we're almost there! (Yeah right, the games we play, smile!) Everybody's used! If you're not useful, you're useless. Thanks for the tombstone. Be safe!

Sheranda, and everybody at Flava's Hair Salon, thanks for keeping me fly, Latricia, Arthur Pless, and Reggie at Slice, thank you for your continued support. You all are true supporter if no one buys a book I know you all will. That means so much to me, Thank you!

In addition, I want to thank Albie and Steve at Cheddar Magazine DVD, Mike at Upscale Entertainment and Dino at Metro Boy Entertainment. Also thanks to all of my friends and family—you know who you are, I love you all!

-Tonetta Chester

Sunshine Through Darkness

Tonetta Chester

Chapter 1

Opening New Doors

"The minute I make it through one door, another opens in its place"

-Neshela

It was Friday, April 20, 2007, and I landed at Newark Liberty International Airport around noon. This was my first trip back to dirty Jersey. Ivan picked me up; we spent three hours riding around the city. I wanted to reminisce, so I asked Ivan to drive me to every location that he had ever taken Jerri and me. He granted my wish and pulled out his little black book. Ivan's book contained every location that he'd ever driven us to, including the dates and times. He kept a detailed log for billing purposes—I was grateful for that.

Jerri, who made all the rules, was no longer alive, so the restrictions that he had previously laid out for me did not apply. I resented some of his stupid rules, but if it meant having him back, I would have gladly followed all of them. I didn't have to use Angela to drive me in the hood, so I had Ivan drive me to Mimi's salon. I hadn't told anyone that I was coming to Jersey, so Mimi was surprised to see me.

"Aw, Neshela! What are you doing here? Why didn't you call me?"

"I wanted it to be a surprise," I told her. We gave each other big hugs.

"It's been so long. You okay?" she asked.

"I'll be okay. It's been hard, but it's time."

"I know," she said. "So when are you going to visit him?"

"Today. I got to talk to him. I miss him, Mimi."

"I know, me too. Your driver brought you here?"

"Oh, shit. I forgot about Ivan."

"Here are the keys, the truck is out front. I know you better be staying with us. You need help with your bags?"

"No, Ivan will do it. Yes, I'm staying with you, Mimi." I always stayed with her when I was in Jersey, even before I met Jerri.

Mimi's best friend Rachel and her cousin Nancy arrived at the salon shortly after; it was like old times. We declared that Saturday would be girls' night out. Even though my trip was for Jerri, I welcomed the invitation. I hadn't partied since my twenty-fifth birthday celebration in Miami at the Forbes. I needed to unwind. It felt good being back in Jersey. I spent Friday evening at Rachel's house. We lay on the floor reminiscing about the good old days. I don't know how we got on the topic of suicide, but it brought tears to my eyes. At that moment, Rachel pulled an aqua-bound book off her shelf, titled *Conversations with God: Book 1, Volume II*. "Neshela, you should look at this one. I completely lost it after my mother died, and this book really touched my soul. It might help you." She handed me the book and exited the room. Without delay, I opened the book and went directly to the index: *suicide*, *death*, *communicating with the dead*, *darkness*, and *love*. After reading each section, I felt like I was finally feeding my soul. I hadn't done this in years.

The weekend flew by. Before I knew it, it was Monday morning. I planned to spend most of the day with Jerri because I hadn't made it to the gravesite on Friday. Feeling guilty, I asked Rachel to drive me to the cemetery so I could be there the minute it opened. I had never been to his gravesite, but I couldn't believe what I was looking at. I was hoping I was at the wrong place; that's how bad it was. They could have buried him anywhere else; shit, they could have buried him in the backyard. The cemetery was located on Central Avenue and Thirteenth Street. Shit couldn't get any worse than this. I wouldn't bury my dog at that cemetery. The grounds were unkempt, the tombstones were covered in graffiti, and the stench that came from the place was horrible. The whole cemetery looked like an afterthought! To make matters worse, Jerri didn't even have a tombstone. A bottle of Patron marked his spot. *Wow.*

After laying two dozen red roses and a mixed spring flower arrangement on his grave, I returned to the office of the cemetery. "I would like to purchase a tombstone for Jerri Hopkins, grave number two, row number fifty-three," I said.

"Well, the prices range from $800 to $1750," the man in the office said, speaking as if he was talking about a lot of money. It was obvious he was used to dealing with penny pinchers.

"I don't care how much it costs. He doesn't have a tombstone and he should, so the price doesn't matter."

"I'm sorry, miss, just a moment. I have to pull the file. What's your name?"

"Neshela Jones."

"I'm sorry, Miss Jones, but I can't sell you a tombstone. Only Mrs. Ilene Hopkins can order it."

"That's fine. Can I just leave the money? You can call his mother and tell her to pick out whatever one she wants. I just want him to have a tombstone."

"Miss, I can't take your money, it's our policy. You will have to contact her and she will have to be here to place the order."

I began to get flustered. "I just want him to have a tombstone, sir."

"I understand, miss, but it's our policy. I'm sorry. You can try calling the funeral service company. They may be able to help you."

I mumbled a thank you in his direction, but I was already dialing the next number I needed. I called Woody Funeral Home and heard the same information. I decided to call Abdul, one of Jerri's closest friends, but he didn't answer. *What a shame*, I thought. *Even if his family can't afford to pay for a tombstone, where the fuck is all these niggas from the block running around, talking about Alpine and The Firm and that Jerri is the mayor? They couldn't come up with $800 for a tombstone, but they could have a R.I.P. party? How soon people forget!*

Abdul called back, and I immediately started yelling, asking why Jerri didn't have a tombstone. "Neshela, his mom didn't buy one. I guess she couldn't afford it."

"I told you months ago that I would pay for the tombstone. Can you call his mother and tell her? I left my number with the cemetery. All she has to do is call and pick the one she wants. Tell her I'll pay for it!"

"I'll call her and I'll call you back." He never did.

It was time to go home, but before I left, I had to make a trip to City Hall to get the documents that I had come to Newark for in the first place. I asked Rachel to give me a ride to City Hall, and when we arrived, I was second in line. Within a matter of minutes, the young woman at the window handed me a sealed envelope that read "Newark Division of Community Health." She instructed me where to get the other document that I'd requested. I didn't bother to unseal the envelope—I already knew the cause of Jerri's death was suicide. I followed the young woman's instructions which led me to the records department.

After ten minutes of going back and forth with the officer behind the bulletproof glass, I became upset. Newark's system is ancient.

"Miss, are you sure you have the right date?"

"Yes, sir. October 30."

"You said it was a suicide, right?"

"Yes, sir. Suicide. And his name is J-E-R-R-I Hopkins."

"Miss," the officer said, "I can't find anything with the information that you're giving me. You have to go upstairs to headquarters."

"Upstairs where?"

The officer quickly spouted off directions, telling me to look for double doors that would lead to headquarters. Sighing, I followed his directions. When I entered the double doors, a female clerk rudely greeted me. I wasn't sure to what her problem was, but I tried my best to ignore her; she knows not what she do. "I just need a copy of a police report," I told her.

"What is the case number?"

"I don't have the case number, ma'am."

"What do you need a copy of the police report for?"

"Excuse me?"

"You're requesting a copy of a homicide report—*what do you need it for?*"

"I'm requesting a copy of a *suicide* report!"

"Records sent you here, right? You want a copy of Jerri Hopkins's report, *right?*"

"Yes!"

"Have a seat. A detective will be right with you."

My heart was racing—a detective, a homicide. *What the hell is she talking about?* I unsealed the envelope and scanned the page. "Box 29. Death due to: Pending investigation."

Oh my God. I am sitting in the lobby of homicide headquarters, and here comes this bitch again.

"*What's* your name again?" she asked.

"Look, I don't have time for this. I have a flight to catch."

"Oh, you have time."

I needed to get the hell out of there. I was just about to curse this bitch out when a male voice interrupted us. "Are you Neshela Jones?"

"Yes, why?"

"Ms. Jones, You have the right to remain silent. If you give up that right, anything you say can and will be used against you in a court of law. You have the right to an attorney and to have an attorney present during questioning. If you cannot afford an attorney, one will be provided to you at no cost. During any questioning, you may decide at any time to exercise these rights, to not answer any questions or make any statements. Do you understand the rights I have just read to you? With these rights in mind, do you wish to speak to me?"

"Excuse me! Sir what are you talking about? Am I under arrest?" Suddenly a woman came storming through the doors demanding to speak with the detective. "My son was killed two days ago and you people have no answers. It was that gang and you know it, detective! You know it!" The detective turned to me. "Ms. Jones, have a seat, I'll be right with you. I need to talk to you. I really want to ask you some questions." This detective had just lost his mind if he thought that I was going to sit here and wait on him to arrest me. I watched him walk the woman towards the back of the police station and when the coast was clear, I bent the corner as fast as my two legs could carry me and down the stairs I went. A million thoughts ran through my mind. *Am I really a suspect in this murder? Do they really think I killed Jerri?* I pushed the door open and ran right into a detective. I didn't even need to see the badge on his chest. He had that detective 'look'—tall, athletic build, bald head.

"Excuse me sir." The reflection from his badge was blinding me.

"No excuse me, gorgeous! What's your name?"

"Ne…Netta." I wasn't about to tell him my real name.

"Well hi, Ms. Netta. I'm Albie. How are you today?"

"I'm in a rush, nice to meet you." I didn't have time to flirt with any man right now.

"We haven't met yet. Here, take my card and call me, beautiful."

"Sure."

I immediately called Rachel on my cell phone. I needed to get to the airport.

"Hello?"

"Meet me at the side door of City Hall. Shit just got crazy!"

"What happened? Are you okay?

"I'll tell you when I get in the car. Hurry up!"

"I'll be right there."

As I exited the doors of City Hall, I looked up thanking God for getting me out. I noticed that I was standing in front of Spain's. This is where it all began. *May 21, 2004.* I remember it clear as day. Jerri and I are walking up the sidewalk. We're following the hostess up the stairs where she seats us at the table right next to the door on the left. I'm looking Jerri up and down out of the corner of my eye. He's wearing a pair of shades with a green, pink and white Ralph Lauren polo. We start a little small talk.

 "Neshela, Neshela!" Rachel shouts. I was so spaced out that I didn't even hear her. "Neshela!" The sirens of the police car quickly remind me that today was April 23, 2007, not May 21, 2004 and Jerri is dead! I jumped into Rachel's truck.

"Neshela, girl, are you okay?"

"Rachel, this shit is crazy. The detective wants to question me about J's murder."

"Murder! I thought he committed suicide."

"So did I!"

"So what did they say?"

"I didn't give him a chance to say anything. After he read me my rights he told me to have a seat. He walked off to help another woman and I walked out."

"Bitch, you crazy! You just walked out?"

"Yeah, I'm good! I wasn't going to sit there and wait for him to arrest me or question me. I don't know anything. Jerri didn't call me! They need to question them hoes he call. I'm not the one. I have to get home. My baby's flight lands at 4:00 pm in Atlanta and I have to be there. I got to get the hell out of here!"

"Wow! This is crazy, what could have happened?"

"I don't know, I just need to get home. I have to make it home for my baby." My mind began to race. *Who killed Jerri and why?*

Chapter 2

Getting the
Hell Out of Newark

"I've always hated dirty Jersey, now I have to escape it like a fugitive"

-Neshela

I boarded Continental flight 1169 to Atlanta. As soon as the flight became airborne, I pulled out the death certificate, hoping to see something different. I write to the only two people that could have known what happened on the early morning of October 30, 2006.

> *Dear God,*
>
> *What have I gotten myself into? I feel like Adam when he ate the forbidden fruit in the Garden of Eden. What do I do? Jerri is gone and Newark police wants to question me. I've been told that you won't put more weight on me than I can bear, but GOD you have really been throwing some heavy weight at me...I can't carry this. I love you, Lord, I just need you to be here with me through it all. I will not lose my faith in you! God, I want to know. Let him talk to me. I know you got him, there is no other place he could be but next to you. He's my angel... he's our angel! God, let him talk to me so that he can tell me what's going on. I need to know what I'm up against.*
>
> *I love you, Lord.*

> *Better Half,*
>
> *Jerri, please tell me what happened. Give me a sign! I need to know... what is going on? Why do they want to question me? Who would implicate me in your murder and why? I wonder, is it Shitara? That bitch couldn't be*

that resentful. I can kill that ho... why the fuck would she put me in the middle of this shit? I heard the stories Jerri, and I ignored them because of you! That's your baby mom and she is playing with my freedom! Baby I need you now more than ever. Talk to me! Talk to me... Jerri talk to me!

It was the longest two hour flight that I ever took. I arrived at the Atlanta airport at 2:20 pm. I had to wait two hours for Astar's flight from Miami so I decided to walk into Hudson Books and pick up a copy of *Conversations with God*. However, they only had Book 3, not Book 1. I needed something to help clear my mind, so I bought it anyway. As I checked out, the cashier gave me a promotional black nylon bag. I went straight to page 121, "Communicating with the Dead." The book said that it was important to pay attention to signs and not to dismiss or ignore them. Within moments the black nylon bag that the cashier had handed me dropped from my shoulder. On the side of the bag was a big red circle with a white dot in the middle. The writing below it scared the hell out of me. *Hopkins Perennial.* I don't know any more—this talking to the dead stuff. My emotions are screwed up. I don't know if I should drop the bag and run or just scream. How crazy will I look? At this moment I sit down and cry; I chose not to ignore the signs.

Astar's flight arrived at 4:00 on the dot. I had never been happier to see my daughter in my life. We took a car service home; it reminded me of Ivan in the old days. Maybe it was just my nerves, but it seemed like the ride home took forever. I called Rachel and Mimi to let them know that I made it home safe. I also called Quan to tell him what had happened. He seemed just as shocked as I was so he agreed that I did the right thing by leaving the police station immediately.

The first few days were rough—I was in a constant state of paranoia. But it had been a week, and thankfully I hadn't heard anything from the Newark police department. I only went out to take Astar to and from school. But after three weeks I came to the conclusion that if Newark police really wanted me, they would have picked my black ass up. I was sure I wouldn't be that hard to find.

As I sat on the bed, I kept thinking about calling the gentlemen that I ran into at City Hall. Since he's a detective, he may be able to give me information about the case. Suddenly my phone rang.

"Hello?"

"Hey Neshela, How are you?"

"Hey Lisa! What's good?"

"Girl just work, I'll be off prevention soon. I'm thinking about coming to Atlanta to see you. How do you like it out there?"

"Atlanta is really starting to grow on me, Lisa. I guess I'm starting to get used to it. I hated this gay-ass city at first! But really beside the huge population of gay, bi and DL brothers, the city is peaceful and quiet. It's not like Miami at all! Plus, everything closes at eleven in the suburbs, even the gas stations, girl! Lisa really, it's the most peaceful place I have ever lived."

"For real? I got to come up there. How are you handling things? "

"I'm okay, I'm just trying to make the best of everything."

"I was just checking on you. Call me if you need to talk. Love ya!"

"Will do, love you too. Bye!"

"Wait, Shela. About all that stuff happening in Jersey, did you call Jeff? Is everything okay?"

"Nothing happened to my knowledge, and I didn't bother to call Jeff."

"Girl, you may want to check on that. At least Jeff can make sure there isn't a warrant out for you."

"I will, Lisa... I will." With those words I hung up. Jeff had represented Lisa and her case, and she got off good. It cost her sixty thousand, but she got off with two years on paper and that's good, considering she was looking at thirty years.

Since the indictment Lisa and I hadn't talked much, but still I would do just about anything for her. I'd known Lisa since 1997. She's good people. The case with my brother was just a fucked up situation. I don't know if we will ever be as close as we once were.

When I pulled up to Astar's school, it was already 2:30 pm. As I came closer to the carpool circle, my eyes scanned through the crowd of kids trying to find Astar. It took a minute, but finally I saw my baby, just as pretty as she can be. She was standing next to two of her classmates twisting her finger through her curly hair. I couldn't help but think of Mrs. Hopkins calling my daughter nappy head! Astar is the most beautiful biracial little girl with the prettiest gray eyes and her hair is naturally curly. It's thick as hell, I must admit, but nappy isn't the word.

We took the scenic route home so that we could enjoy nature. It was our first spring in Georgia and considering that Miami only has one season, summer, we were enjoying every minute of spring and the greenish-yellow fog that it brought. After we finished homework, I began to prepare Astar's favorites: chicken, macaroni and cheese, and green beans. A few hours after dinner, I got Astar ready for bed while I got myself together for the first episode of the new season of *The Wire*.

The following day I finally called my attorney David Jeff. Jeff had represented me before on a felony battery case back in 2002. Of course we won, and I stayed out of trouble after that. For this reason, Jeff was a little surprised to hear from me. I explained what happened when I was in Jersey. He said that he was licensed to practice in New Jersey and he would represent me if I needed him, but he suggested that I call the detective who wanted to question me. He said that it was probably nothing to worry about because his assistant couldn't find any warrant for my arrest. Jeff told me to call him back on his private cell if I needed him or if the detective said anything out of the ordinary. I was happy that he was going to represent me if I needed him because he was one of the best lawyers in South Florida.

Even with all the mouth in the world and being the bad bitch that I am, I couldn't stomach calling the police department. I began to look for the card of the man that I had run into that day at City Hall. I found it in the bottom of one of my Gucci bags: Sergeant Albert Bashire. I started to call and then changed my mind. Even if he was just trying to holla at me, his instinct is to be aware. I would need to have seduction and power to stay two steps ahead of him. I knew a lot about both. Jerri and I had read the book *48 Laws of Power* a few times. I bought it for him a few years back. *The Power of Seduction* was one of my all-time favorites. The book truly teaches a woman to get what she wants.

It took a day to finalize my plan. I had my lawyer on call. I planned to be completely honest with the sergeant. I dialed his number with no hesitation.

"Hello?" he said in a deep voice.

"Hey, may I speak with Albie?"

"May I ask who's calling?"

"Sure, I guess I can tell you who I am!"

"I'm listening."

"My name is Neshela but they call me Netta." I had to clear the first lie about my name.

"Oh, I remember you! Pretty little thang that ran into me a few weeks ago. Right?"

"Yes!"

"I just got in the office, can I call you right back? Give me 15 minutes."

"Sure."

He surprised me when he actually called me back. I guess he saved my number from the caller ID. We talked for a while and he told me a lot about himself. He had been divorced for over ten years and had two daughters and one son. I almost didn't believe him when he said he was forty-six because he had the body of a twenty year old. Before we hung up we made a promise to keep in touch.

The very next day Albie called again. We spoke on a regular basis for the next week. I was waiting for him to ask me what I was doing in City Hall. This was the only point in talking to him. I wanted to know about the case, and I planned to ask him when the time was right. I was just waiting for him to ask me the question I needed.

Albie appeared to be a nice guy, and I enjoyed talking to him, but I really just wanted to know what was going on with Jerri's case. This was the beginning of a new thing.

Chapter 3

Life

"God grant me the serenity to accept the things I cannot change; courage to change the things I can; and wisdom to know the difference."

-Reinhold Niebuhr

After Jerri died I had no one in Atlanta except for a distant cousin and Malik's chick Melissa. Tamika, a friend of my brother's girlfriend, was another new friend of mine. She was cool at first, but the bitch turned out to be messy. Besides, her and my ex Christopher had some funny business going on. She didn't appear to be his type, but pussy is pussy. You know how that goes, so I kept my distance. It seems that Atlanta is the new hot spot, but I never had to worry about running into anyone from the crib. I lived fifty minutes north of the city, so I didn't go there that much. I usually never go any further than Buckhead and I only went there to shop at Phipps Plaza or Lenox Mall.

Astar had horse riding lessons twice a week and her Saturday lesson lasted for two and a half hours, so Melissa and I met at the mall. My weekends at the mall had ended some time ago. I had to come to the tough realization that my sponsor had died. Going into Gucci to spend G's wasn't on the top of my to-do list. Maybe a G but definitely not three or four. Besides, I had more than enough shit. But I still enjoyed my time with Melissa. She was cool as shit and one of the realist bitches that I have been around in a minute. She was older than me, but she was in a similar situation when her dude got locked up back in the 90s. It was the case of the eighteen realist niggas. Long story short, they all got off after three years. She was one of the only wives that was able to hold on to everything. This is not common for street niggas; most of the time when a street nigga dies or goes to jail, the repo man comes and picks up everything. It usually doesn't take more than six months, and the hustler's wife has moved on to the next hustler. Most of the time it's a friend that was always around. There were only a few women that knew how to hold things down. Melissa and my uncle Sed's wife were the two women that

I admired when it came to this. These bitches had their shit together, and I respected them for it.

After an hour of shopping with Melissa, I was done! I had already spent five hundred dollars over my shopping budget for the month. This was why I only went to the mall with her every other month. Melissa will have me going broke, and she has this way of making you feel like you don't know what you're doing. "Girl, you got to learn how to shop." Melissa always said this and I never understood it. Finally, I asked her what the hell that meant.

"Shela, you just pick up shit! You have to learn how to shop! You not with J, and in fact it ain't no nigga at the register with you paying for your shit, girl! Let me be the bearer of bad news— you not going to get a nigga here, definitely not a thousand nigga. Not in Atlanta, they don't exist anymore! You out there with the crackers in Alpharetta, so you better try and get you a white boy! Anyway, what you want to eat?"

"It doesn't matter girl. Let's just eat Twist, since we right here." Melissa had me thinking, it's been a minute since I put some thought into the fact that I was single and living in gay-ass Atlanta. To make matters worse, women outnumber men 17 to 1 in Atlanta, and 10 out of the 17 are beautiful women just like me.

After the mall, I went to pick up Astar, but I had totally forgotten that it was a sleep over retreat at the ranch where Astar had her riding lessons. It was another lonely night for me; I pulled out the package that Rachel had sent me two months ago. The box read, "Give your climax the golden touch!" I called Rachel to get instructions because I never played with myself. I thought it was nasty, like anal sex and cum in your mouth. Some shit is off limits for me. I hadn't had sex since Jerri, and we had enough sex to hold me over for at least another six months. Still, I was lonely. I put the Golden Bullet on my clit and turned the speed all the way up. This had to be the best invention ever. I came over and over again. I was hooked. It reminded me of the first time Jerri licked my ass.

When I woke up, the bullet was lying right next to me. I jumped in the shower and brushed my teeth. I oiled my body down and put on a pair of True Religion jeans with a white Ed Hardy tank top. Then my cell phone rang.

"Hey, Albie, what's going on?"

"Hello, lady, how are you?"

"I just got out of the shower."

"I'm just sitting here thinking about you. I would love to have lunch or dinner with you. Or breakfast... I just want to see you. Can you send me a picture?"

"Go to my MySpace. I have lots of pictures on there. "

"When are you coming back to Jersey?"

"Never. I hate Newark."

"Hold on Ms. Lady, this is my city!" As if that was supposed to mean something to me. "So what were you doing in City Hall that day?'

Finally, I thought.

"I thought I told you my dude died last year and I was just getting a copy of a document for the insurance company."

"Your boyfriend got killed in Newark?" He fell right into the trap.

"I don't know if he was killed or just died."

"What does the police report say? What precinct? Do you have the case number?"

"I never found out. The bitch in Homicide was acting like an asshole so I just left!"

"What was her name?"

"I don't know! She was rude as hell."

"You should have told me, I could have gotten it for you. What was your boyfriend's name and when did it happen?"

"J-E-R-R-I Hopkins. October 30, 2006. They said it was a suicide."

"Let me look into it."

"Okay I'll be home."

"Okay, baby girl I'll call you a little later. I'm going to look into it.

"Please do, I've been dying to know! Sometimes I wish his mother and I had a better relationship."

"Don't worry about it. You can't make anyone like you. You ain't her type anyway. That's how hood mothers are."

I felt like I was making progress. I couldn't wait for Albie to call back. I needed to know what really happened. I stayed in the house patiently waiting, but he didn't call. Three hours later I was driving to pick up Astar. I was getting caught at every red light, and I saw that I was being followed. I switched lanes to get a look. "Damn. What the… " It was just some white woman with a dog and two kids in the back seat. Damn, I guess I was just paranoid. I made it to the ranch just in time to see the girls do their last run and groom the horses. On the way home I stopped at the same traffic light and asked Astar to read me the street sign. "Mommy, it said Alpine! You can't see it?"

"No, the sun's in my eyes." This little girl already had a mouth. When we got home, I called Albie back. "How was your day?"

"Good! I was going to call you from the office. I just want to talk about this on a recorded line because it's procedure."

"Okay."

Within seconds, he called me back. He said Jerri's suicide appeared to be a murder. The police report stated that several shots had been fired from three different guns and several different gun shells had been found in the car, which was puzzling to me. The autopsy report stated that the gunshot wound that killed Jerri was self-inflicted, which was even crazier. If Jerri killed himself, why were three different gun shells found in the car? I couldn't ignore the evidence—even Albie said that they should be investigating this case as a homicide because of unusual circumstances.

Albie gave me a quick lesson in body counts. At the end of the day, if Jerri's family didn't stand up and demand that Newark police department solve the case, it would be closed as a suicide. This meant that there would be no case to solve, which meant the body count would stay down. The current murder rate in Newark was so high it was bringing negative publicity to the city, so Jerri's case would be one less murder in the books if it was considered a suicide. Albie also told me that there was a statement given about the relationship I had with Jerri. He said my name was listed as a person of interest. He told me not to worry about it, and for now the case was just sitting, waiting to be closed out. But Jerri didn't have anyone fighting for him. His family wasn't trying to figure out what really happened and who could have done this. I don't know, maybe they were afraid that what happened to him could possibly happen to them, so it was better to leave it alone. Newark police considered the case a suicide. The conversation left me mad at the world.

I had no plans to talk to Albie again. He's a nice guy and all, but he's still a cop, and I don't fuck with the police.

Chapter 4

Party Time

"We used to party our ass off on South Beach"

-Neshela

The NJ Boys were coming to the A to party. I hadn't partied in ages. Melissa and I would go to Justin's restaurant for Martini Monday's every now and then, but seeing as we ditched our bill a few weeks ago, we needed a break. Still, I was happy to be going out again.

I was stuck in traffic on my way to the airport to pick up Quan, Mack and the crew. I had been on 85 South next to the 17th Street exit looking at Atlantic Station for 20 minutes. I hate being late to pick up people.

Quan called. "Shela, you're taking too long! We're going to take a cab to the hotel."

"Okay, Quan, I'm sitting in traffic on 85. I haven't moved in 40 minutes."

"The traffic crazy like that?"

"Wait until y'all get on the expressway!"

"Meet us at the hotel. Where you want to eat?"

"There's a Ruth's Chris and a Houston's across from the hotel."

"Alright! See you at the hotel."

Good thing the traffic isn't so bad going north. They still beat me to the hotel, but I made it just in time for dinner. Houston's was our pick. Doman, one of the New Jersey boys, had all the jokes. "Shela your man coming, he'll be here in a few hours!" Everyone burst out laughing. He was talking about Wesley, which was an ongoing joke with all of them.

"That shit ain't funny! Fuck you, Doman! Whatever." Everyone continued to laugh while Doman imitated Wesley. Doman's funny as hell, and I couldn't help but laugh. Just when I thought it was over, Mack and Quan jumped in with a few more jokes. After dinner I went home to get ready for the night. I called Melissa to meet us at the Compound.

Compound was one of Atlanta hot spots, so we had to be there. I jumped in my BMW 525i and headed to the hotel to round up the boys. I was thinking it shouldn't take more than 20 minutes to get to the hotel in Buckhead. It was already 11 so I had to hurry. The club closed at 3! I called Quan to let him know I was on the way. I got to the hotel at about a quarter past. Melissa called to tell me she was almost at the club, so I redirected her to the hotel. While Mack was still looking for something to wear, Doman started in again with the Wesley jokes.

"Neshela, your homeboy just made it! He came all the way here to see you."

"Whatever, Mr. Funny Man! You do need a ride to the club."

"I'll get there, even if I have to ride with your boyfriend."

Quan walked in the door just in time because I was about to chew Doman up. I was sick of the jokes. "Mack's ready y'all, let's get out of here," Quan said. We met Melissa in the lobby. "There go your boy!" Doman said in a soft voice.

I rolled my eyes and felt anger boiling up. "My man is dead and I would appreciate it if you would not call him as a boy. Cause a man is what he was!" Doman just looked at me and didn't say another word.

We arrived at the Compound at 1:00 am, and after valet parking the cars we walked straight to the front. After passing security, it took us a second to decide which VIP section we were going to make our home for the night. Compound had everything from techno to hip-hop. It's a sleek, modern space designed to deliver a range of sensory experiences—truly sexy. We chose the Ride room at the back. It was the largest room in the club and had a VIP section. The hostess greeted us and took our drink orders.

The VIP section began to fill up fast, and with all of the other people, it started to become a party.

Melissa whispered, "There go your man." There was Allan Iverson and his entourage. I just love him! I admired him from afar, but then Doman started blocking my view. "Move, Doman!"

"Let's dance!"

"Get out my way." I moved my head side to side trying to see A.I. Doman finally realized that I was trying to look at my man.

"You groupie, get out here." We both burst out laughing.

The DJ announced, "Good night Atlanta, it's time to get out!" With those words, the lights turned on. The DJ continued to give club shout outs as security began to sweep the areas. I never even heard him make the last call.

"Shit, it's over like that," Wesley said, looking at me like I worked at the club. He had been standing next to me the whole night.

"I told y'all shit close early down here."

"It's only 2:45!" Wesley exclaimed.

"Yeah I know." I had to end the small talk. I was doing a good job of ignoring him. Wesley had no idea that I knew all the stories he told. I had wanted to call him out for the corny ass nigga he was ever since Shelly, Quan's sister, told me that shit when we were in Atlantic City last summer. As my uncle would say, let a nigga think you don't know shit, treat them the same, then kill him.

Wesley was my nigga, but he tried to play me out and that shit was fucked up regardless of how he felt about J. J never said anything about him and neither had I. I accepted Wesley for who he was, like I do with all people. But I hate liars, and real friends don't play each other out. Hi and bye are the only words we will ever share now.

I began to chant, "Pop, lock, and drop it, pop, lock, and drop it! Y'all Jersey niggas was doing the down south shit." Quan and Doman had me dying laughing. They were really pop, lock, and dropping it. We were still laughing as we walked to the car; it was an early night. After making sure everyone got to the hotel, Melissa and I raced to highway 400 seeing who would make it home first.

The following day we did the mall thing. This was a normal part of the NJ Boys' trip. After the mall we all went to DASS Spa at Lenox. I hadn't been to the spa since Jerri died. I had made our appointment to the spa as part of Jerri's birthday gift, but we never made it, so this spa visit was difficult for me. I exhaled, thinking that I was supposed to be with Jerri, but instead it's Quan, Mack, and Doman. It's going to be an hour of pain regardless of how well the masseuse works out the kinks. I can only think of my Saturdays at Shore Hill, and how I would come home to Jerri and Neiman Marcus bags. All the memories play over and over again. I miss him so much.

The NJ Boys had to get back to Jersey and I had to get back to my boring life. I was a true soccer mom with no husband. I woke up every morning at 6:30. I dropped Astar off at school at 7:40 and then I went to Barnes & Noble to read. I always ordered a hot cocoa at Starbucks. Once a week I would have lunch with Astar at her school. I prepared dinner Sunday through Thursday, and we ate at 6:30 pm. After dinner we took our showers because bedtime was at 8:00 pm for Astar and 9:30 pm for me. My new life! No shopping sprees, no drama, no trips, just peace and boredom.

At least that was what I thought until Ghost, a family friend with whom I'd had a secret affair, called, telling me to met him at the airport. He said he needed to talk to me. When I arrived at the airport, I called Ghost. He told me to meet him at Houlihan's on the second floor. He was sitting at a table in the back of the restaurant looking sexy as ever. I hadn't seen him in years. I never forgave him for getting married without telling me. We had been through so much. It hurt me that he didn't share the news of his marriage, and when he denied it, it hurt me more. We had been close for as long as I could remember, sharing stories about everything that went on. Part of me still loved him, and I was happy to see him.

"How are you holding up?" he asked. The question caught me off guard. He asked about my finances. I told him I had about $40,000 left. At the end of our conversation he told me if I wanted to close on my house and move in, I could. He also told me that he would support me financially. All that he asked in return was that I go back to school full time. I sat at the table, knowing that this was the end of our friendship. I felt so disrespected. He was married now, and that changed everything for me. I got up from the table and said, "Ghost, I have to go. I got everything under control and I'm going to look for a job soon. Thanks anyway." As bad as I wanted to slap the shit out of him, I chose not to. Ghost had been good to me and I truly believe he was just trying to help me. But playing second was never my thing, even if the price was good.

Chapter 5

MySpace

"It seems all these new social networks are a way to reconnect with your past"

-Neshela

I was sitting on my couch checking my MySpace page. A little girl had requested to be my friend. I was a little puzzled, but I sent a nice message back:

Neshela Jones: Hello sweetie. I'm not sure that I know you. Do I know u from NJ? Or are you just asking to be my friend?

Nieci Hopkins: I'm J's little sister Nieci.

Neshela Jones: Oh, baby girl how are you? How is school? How are your mom and Red, and Jason, how is he? Hope you all are okay. Call me sometime!

Nieci Hopkins: I'm okay, everybody is fine. And I will call you sometime! How are you and Astar doing?

Neshela Jones: We're okay. By the way, how did you find me?

Nieci Hopkins: U sent a comment to a boy that's a friend of my friend.

Neshela Jones: Oh lol! Okay Mack's son, it's a small world.

Nieci Hopkins: When is the next time u coming up here? J's wife Shitara and I needed to ask u some questions.

Neshela Jones: Is this really J's little sister sending this message? I didn't know Jerri got married! LMAO I just got back from Jersey. I usually visit Jerri's grave every few months. I'm not sure if I'm coming next month. What is it that you and Shitara have questions about? You (and/or) Shitara can call me. I'll be up for a while tonight.

(God, grant me the SERENITY to accept the things I cannot change; the COURAGE to change the things I can; and the WISDOM to know the difference. —Reinhold Niebuhr)

Nieci Hopkins: Yea that was Shitara. This is really J's little sister now. And yea she said they got married at city hall a few months before my brother's death. And she just had their second baby girl. What is that comment that you sent me supposed to mean?

Neshela Jones: Exactly what it says! It's just a quote that I live by; I happened to see it on one of those quote websites. Read it so that you understand. It's a great philosophy.

Nieci Hopkins: Thanx I might start living by that philosophy too. Tell your baby girl I said hey and I miss her bad self!

Neshela Jones: Astar said hi too and that she's still waiting on you to braid her hair. She asked if you can tell Jason that she said hello. I'm still curious to know what you and Shitara wanted to talk to me about.

Nieci Hopkins: LOL I will when I come down there for Thanksgiving and I'll tell him. And it was Shitara that wanna talk to u, not me! That was her sending those earlier messages.

Neshela Jones: You're coming to the A for thanksgiving? We look forward to seeing you... Anyway she never called. Maybe this was her way of telling me she had the baby... good for her!! The married thing was funny ;-) LMAO Anyway be good...

Nieci Hopkins: U think that it's funny J and I got married. I'll see u when u come up here to visit J. How are the twins? LOL

Neshela Jones: OK y'all keep confusing ME! Who is this now? I am guessing Shitara!!
About the twins, I guess Jerri didn't tell you I had a miscarriage. And if he did, I don't get the LOL because there's nothing funny about losing two kids... First you had questions to ask me... Now you want to see me.... Do you know what you want? Because you're confusing me! What do you really want? I sent you my number!

FYI Jerri O. Hopkins was never married!

So YES I thought it was real funny that you went out of your way to tell me that you got married to a dead man or to tell me that you had a baby... to be completely honest with you I DON'T give a fuck... I wish you the best because I'm sure it's hard raising two kids without a man. Congrats on your new baby, if that's the truth.

Nieci Hopkins: This is Nieci now. Shitara will message u later about the message u just sent.

Neshela Jones: Y'all are funny!!!! She doesn't need to send me anything. In fact, tell her DON'T. Let's make this our last email. I don't have time to play games.

Nieci Hopkins: Hold up I'm not Shitara or anyone else. I may be young but I don't play with my brother's ex girlfriends. Both of you just stop because I really don't care.

Neshela Jones: ....I don't have time to play with you sweetheart!

Playing is for children and that's not my thing so you won't ever have the opportunity to play with me!! Like I said before, THERE IS NO NEED FOR YOU OR SHITARA to send me anything!!!

This shit has gone a little too far... When you allow people to use you and put you in the middle of their MESS, that's where you'll stay—in the middle of their MESS... NIECI.

If I'm not mistaken, you allowed Shitara to use your MySpace to email me some bullshit (You are a CHILD and children are easily influenced!)

Out of respect and love for Jerri I have been very courteous. But ASK yourself a question—If Jerri was alive would you have DARED????

You know NOT what you do; you still have a lot of growing up to do.

(God, grant me the SERENITY to accept the things I cannot change; the COURAGE to change the things I can; and the WISDOM to know the difference. —Reinhold Niebuhr)

I wish you the best on this journey called LIFE! SERENITY; COURAGE; WISDOM........

Nieci Hopkins: LOL.....SAY NO MORE

I logged off of MySpace and took a deep breath, trying to rid my mind of all the bullshit I just went through. Minutes later, my phone rang and a private number appeared. I figured it wasn't important but I answered it anyway. "Hello?"

"May I speak to Neshela?"

"Who's this?"

"Is this Neshela... Neshela, you always wanted what I had. He married me before he died and I just had our daughter, Heaven. Your run was short—I'm his wife! I can't wait to kick your ass, I wish you would die, bitch. You got some nerve to call me ugly! I can't wait to see you," Shitara shouted.

I watched the seconds on my phone; I can't believe this little dirty-ass girl is calling me out. This bitch didn't even exhale. She said all that shit in less than 10 seconds.

"Look, I don't have time to sit on the phone with this bullshit. Jerri is dead." With those words, I hung up. I didn't bother wasting my breath. She was just the trash that my nigga loved. I guess she had more on her mind because the bitch kept calling. I just pressed the ignore button; I had better shit to do. But she wouldn't stop calling. It reminded me of the days when she'd call Jerri one hundred times. Her finger had to be hurting; 10 minutes later my phone was still ringing.

Finally my phone stopped ringing, and within seconds my phone alerted me that I had a voicemail. This has to be the funniest shit. This bitch left me a message. "Neshela, you always wanted what I had. Tell Mimi I said I'm going to beat her ass for you!"

This bitch was stupid as hell. This nigga was building me a $600,000 house and she wanted to play games with me on MySpace. Now she's married to his corpse, this silly ho and a baby. Wow. This shit never ceases to amaze me.

I looked at the phone in disbelief. This bitch had been a seasonal security guard at a school. She lived in the projects and didn't even have a car. On top of that, she had two kids that look just like J! She got to be joking; she might as well jump off a fucking bridge with that fucked up life! Someone really needs to give her a dose of common sense. This ho's eyes sit across her head like E.T. Ugly motherfucker! Now I said it, 'cause truly I have never called her anything other than his black-ass baby mom or the project chick. I was not really into calling bitches ugly. Beauty is in the eye of the beholder. But this bitch needs a reminder: she had been second to me and every other bitch he's fucked with for as long as I knew him. And about my run being short, stupid ass girl, my short run was much better than your years of being number two. That's what happened when you started out. You've been second and you will always keep that place no matter how many kids you push out of your pussy, stupid bitch! This nigga been dead for a year and I was still living off his money. You live in a room! Stop playing! Saying that I want what you had... this chick is crazy! I guess she doesn't remember that ass-whooping she wore. This bitch ain't got shit! And for the record, my babies were planned—can you say the same? I have so many good memories with Jerri, I could write a book about it!

This bitch just pissed me off with this bullshit. Now I have to call Mimi and tell her to be watchful. I don't know what this ghetto bitch is up to and I would hate for anything to happen to Mimi on account of me. I know Mimi can hold her own but my girl can't wear no scars for me. I was not with that shit! I wish she would call me back. I don't play about my money or my family, and Mimi was my family.

Mimi called me back and I told her about the voicemail. I called Mimi to let her hear the voicemail. God knows I didn't want to but I can't keep her in the dark. After playing the message I didn't bother to stay on the phone with Mimi. Mimi isn't beat about the bullshit and I was glad she didn't feed into it. Still, I was pissed.

I got dressed and walked out the door trying to choose which car I wanted to drive. All I could think about was this silly bitch talking about getting at my girl. This ho ain't even got a car, what she gonna catch the bus to fight a bitch about me? Lord help her! I decide to drive my Jaguar. As I pulled out of the gate of my complex, I opened my sunroof and turned up the radio. My song, "Anonymous," by Bobby V was on.

I needed a shopping spree to make up for this day. I went to the bank where I had two safety deposit boxes. After Jerri died, I took the money out of the house. One box had his money and the other had the money that I accumulated while I was with him and all of my personal savings. I don't know why I kept the money separate because it's all my money now. I went to the box with Jerri's money, took out 6 G's and then called Melissa to meet me at Phipps. I had to treat myself.

Melissa and I had become cool, and, like most of my friends, she could tell when something wasn't right.

"Girl what's wrong with you?" she asked, as if I was doing something unusual.

"Ain't nothing wrong with me!' I said.

"Last month you were bitching about spending two grand and now you acting like you got a black card! Why you ain't telling me Stella got her groove back! Who is the new dude and where is his brother?"

"New dude! I didn't see no dude. Fuck these niggas!"

She turned her head in slow motion toward me, as if I said something so radical. "What's wrong with you? Don't get up here with that gay shit. What the fuck is going on?"

At dinner I told Melissa about Shitara's baby. After Jerri died, I heard stories about a few chicks claiming to be pregnant, but there was no truth to the stories. Even Monique, Quan's baby mom, claimed to be pregnant. We sat at the table trying to figure the whole thing out. Jerri died in October and the baby was just born. She must have gotten pregnant in September or October; Jerri wouldn't have known about her pregnancy.

As mad as I wanted to be, I couldn't help thinking if he had known he would still be here. Would he have made a better choice that day? Jerri loved his kids; Jason and Charm were still here. I thought of the psychic in Atlantic City and how she said Jerri would be the father of three kids. After I lost the twins, I never put any thought into it. Shitara's new baby makes three: Jason, Charm and Heaven.

Chapter 6

Learn to Love Atlanta

"Atlanta, the city of black people. The New Hollywood as they say"

-Neshela

Things were going good, except I was running out of money. I had $138,000 when Jerri died. After I paid $54,000 to take care of all the bills for one year and the $18,000 toward the house, I was left with $66,000. Now I had to start budgeting because I was single and without an income. I needed to find a job. The 6 G's I wasted at the mall last weekend didn't help.

I began to think about Ghost's offer. Unlike most people, anything less than 50 G's is what I considered being broke, and I was damn near there. If I took Ghost's offer I wouldn't have to worry, but that would go against everything that I believed in. He's married! I have more than enough experience to get a good job. I just have to do it. For the next few weeks I job searched, and eventually I was offered positions with Office Depot and a software company. Both positions were on a sales team, but I chose the software company because it was closer to my house, the salary was good, and the commissions were uncapped. It was just the type of job I needed.

The first few weeks of work were a challenge. I hadn't had to report to a job in years and I didn't have to be friendly and sociable with a lot of people. My goal was to stick around for at least two years and save a little money. But first, I had to make it through job training. The training class was a lot harder than I imagined—the instructor was lecturing us and handing out tests every day like we were in graduate school. I barely finished the test and needed a 90 to be hired. I wished I had taken the job with Office Depot.

After three long weeks, I finished the training with an 89, but the instructor hired me anyway because she saw how hard I was working. I was so happy, but two days after I got out of training my supervisor got fired. I heard that he was fucking the boss and then she got emotional and fired him. Who knows with her funny-acting ass, but she was way too emotional to be in management anyway. To make matters worse, now I had to report directly to her.

The first few weeks I dressed my ass off and kept my nose in the sky and out of everyone's business. This working shit was so not for me. It's not even the work—it was dealing with people and their personalities. I was cool with the chick that sat next to me; she and the dude that sat behind me taught me everything I knew. But my favorite person at my new job was my acting supervisor Kevin, a gay guy that I just loved. He was an angel that I had to meet. I'll never forget the day I interviewed with him. Everything was going smoothly, we were just talking about random shit, and all of a sudden he said, "When the student is ready, the teacher will appear." I started crying because I had just written down the same phrase on a sticky note a day earlier and placed it on my bathroom mirror.

It took a while, but I finally started to get used to the job thing. Kevin always came to my desk and we started talking more and more. He had short black hair and caramel-colored skin. He was good-looking and had a lean build because of all the marathons he ran. When he interviewed me, I thought he was married because he was wearing a gold wedding band. He was an effeminate dude, but I had a cousin just like him and he swore he was straight. Kevin later told me that the ring was actually a commitment ring between him and his partner. He also said he had two kids from his first marriage to a woman! I wondered if his kids knew he was gay.

I was starting to get out of the house. I went to Slice on Peter Street and sometimes Mbar. I met a few professional men: a principal, a doctor, and a marketing analyst. I was beginning to love Atlanta! After finally getting out of the house, I was enjoying everything that the city offered.

Over the summer I hung out in the A. I had my swagger back. I had a few dudes on my team, but nothing to brag about. Melissa warned me that thousand-dollar niggas don't exist in Atlanta. This chick at my job hooked me up with her brother. She thought he was my type. He was cool as hell, definitely good people, but he didn't spend enough, and I didn't think I could get used to that shit. With the economy going downhill, niggas ain't spending no more.

Atlanta makes it easy for a nigga to look like he's balling. Most niggas stay in Henry Country or by the airport in an area called Camp Creek where houses only cost $150,000. Big ass four- and five-bedroom houses. These niggas look like they're doing it but they ain't really doing shit. My rent is higher than the mortgages of most of the niggas I talk to.

I refused to settle so I split my time between two or three niggas. My auntie told me once that no man is perfect and at the end of the day they all fuck up. Her motto is, "I'd rather be crying in the back of a limousine than at a bus stop." Uncle Sed said, "As long as you have a pussy, you shouldn't want for anything." He had a point. He didn't mean stand on a corner and sell your pussy. It simply means if you're fucking a nigga you should have what you want. A man should provide for his woman. These were the two rules that I lived by.

Hustlers don't respect money. It comes fast and goes faster. It's hard to get used to fucking with a regular nigga after being a hustler wife. With a hustler, you just ask for something and the money magically appears. With a regular nigga, you ask for the same things over and over and if it's more than a few hundred dollars you're going to have to wait a week or two. If you never fuck with a hustler, good. Then you won't expect so much from a hard-working man. You won't be used to having everything. But one bad decision can fuck up your life forever. Jerri made it hard for me to date. But I guess most men that I dated in the past were good to me. I've been blessed!

The summer came to an end, which meant that Astar would be home tomorrow. She spent every summer in Miami with her pappy, but this was the first year that I would miss her birthday. Since he only got to see her for the summer and holidays, I let him have this year. Besides, it was the first year that Jerri had been gone and it wasn't it any easier that the anniversary of his death was Astar's birthday.

We spent the weekend getting Astar's school supplies. Astar decided she wanted to play the flute, so we also had to stop by a music store. When we arrived at the shopping plaza where the music store was, I saw the line of soccer moms outside. I thought I had been smart by coming early. I guess they thought the same thing.

After two hours of waiting, we finally had everything. It took us a little longer because I had to act like a fool. Sometimes living in Alpharetta as a black woman was difficult. These crackers would just look over you as if you were not there. So every now and then I had to act like a bitch and stick my nose in the sky. My money is green just like everyone else's, so I demanded respect.

I went to the market to get lunch meat for Astar's lunches. She didn't like school lunches so I had to pack lunch every day. I had missed doing all the mom stuff with my daughter. Last year I would surprise her with Burger King for lunch. I would go on all of her field trips because I had so much free time. But now with my new job, I wouldn't be able to. I still planned to do as much as possible.

September flew by and Astar did so well in school. Horse camp was going well, and I was so happy she had adjusted to life in Georgia. I wish I could say the same about myself; it had been a rough year and sometimes I missed Jerri more than I could bear. I hoped he finally had a tombstone, but in the back of my mind I knew he didn't.

Chapter 7

Going Back to Jersey

"Why? I hate this place"

-Neshela

Tonetta Chester

I took flight 1202 to Newark for Lil Quan's christening. Ivan picked me up. The Fairmount Cemetery was my first stop. Instead of a Patron bottle, a teddy bear and some fake flowers marked his spot. Still no tombstone. I didn't let it bother me. I guess my money was too good, or they had too much pride to let me pay for it. I left two dozen white roses and told Ivan to drop me off at Mimi's salon. I hated the fact that it was October and a year had already passed by.

When I reached the salon, Mimi had a few clients so I just sat around laughing at Tracy, one of the stylists. After an hour, I had to get out. I asked Mimi if she wanted something to eat. "Neshela, J used to bring me soup from some place, do you know where it's at? I have been wanting some of that soup for the longest time." I knew exactly where I could find the soup: Elizabeth Ave right by Alpine. When I got there the place was closed.

It was a beautiful day so I drove around Newark. As I jammed to Keyshia Cole, I realized that I missed dirty-ass Newark. I was riding down Bloomfield Avenue, looking at all the familiar things and missing the hell out of Jerri. I drove by our house on 6th Street and the tears began to flow. Mona, our neighbor, was standing outside. I pulled the truck to the side right in front of her to speak to her. We greeted each other with big hugs. Mona soon had me laughing about the game we used to play: Jerri and I would hear her and Steve making love and we would go at it just to see who could make the most noise.

After leaving 6th street I went back to the cemetery to talk to Jerri. The white roses that I had left were gone. I talked to J for a little over twenty minutes, but I saw the cemetery was closing, so

I wrapped up my chat. Still thinking of J, I headed back to Mimi's salon.

That evening I went to the Garden State Mall with Dale, one of Mimi's friends, and her son. I still hadn't eaten. Our first stop was the California Pizza Kitchen. By the time the server got to the table I was starving. I ordered a chicken Caesar sandwich and raspberry lemonade. Dale and her son were still undecided but I advised the server to put my order in because I had to eat!

Dale was even worse than Mimi when it came to shopping. Dale is slow as hell; she has an eye for good stuff, but my God! By the time we got back to the salon Mimi was finishing her last customer. I was tired. I wanted to go to Mimi's house and dive into bed.

Before I knew it, Quan was waking us up. We couldn't be late for the christening. It was still dark outside. It was too damn early for me, so I crawled back into bed and pulled the covers over my head.

By the time I got up, Mimi had already changed four times. I only brought two outfits. We made it out of the house just in time to pick up Lil Quan from his Aunt Shelly. After getting the baby dressed, we headed to the church. All seventy of us took up one whole side of the church.

Lil Quan ran around the church as if he was going to preach. He was wearing a little white suit. Not even the pastor could ignore him. After the ceremony we all met up at Niece's and South Organ for dinner. I sat next to Rachel at the table near the door. Wesley, Mack and Tammy sat at the table next to us. Wesley shouted out to us, "Y'all better come and sit next to daddy, so y'all can laugh." I knew they were going to be talking about everyone like they always did.

I wanted to spit in his face. Like I'm going to sit next to Wesley's ass! "Y'all crazy," I said. "I'm not fucking with y'all today. We just left church!" Mack, Wesley and Tammy just laughed.

"Yeah, y'all might want to stay over there 'cause this the table that nobody likes," Wesley said. He was right. Despite everything that happened between Mack's girl Tammy and Mimi, Quan and Mack were still close, but nobody liked Tammy.

Everyone began to line up to get something to eat. I received a text message from a New Jersey number that I didn't know. *"I know you had something to do with his death."*

I texted back, *"Who is this?"*

"You know what happened, you know! Bitch."

I was angry and hurt at the same time. I truly loved this man and to be accused of his death hurt. The texts kept coming. *"I know you're in Jersey and your flowers are in the garbage."* This bitch was crazy. Rachel turned to me and asked me what was wrong.

I knew it had to be Shitara. "It's J's baby mom." I showed Rachel the texts.

"Damn, those are some serious accusations," Rachel said. It was time to put an end to this bullshit.

I texted her back, *"I really want to know why you feel this way. My number won't change. When you grow up and want to talk like a woman you got the number."* Rachel couldn't believe that my message was so nice. I went to the restroom to pull myself together. On my way back I ran into Quan. I tried to cover my face, but he saw the tears anyway. I told him about the texts. He put his arm around my shoulder and told me to change my number and not to worry. I was feeling him, but I was not changing my number for this stupid bitch.

After the christening we all went to see *Why Did I Get Married?*, Tyler Perry's new movie. It was truly like the old days, before there was a Jerri, before Wesley started fronting, before Mimi and Rochelle's drama, before all the bullshit. I used to just come to Jersey to get away from the drama in Miami. We used to watch movies all the time.

The next morning I went back to Atlanta. The house was empty because Astar was in Miami visiting her grandmother whom she called *abuela* and her pappy. Melissa was also in Miami. I don't really like Atlanta, but I didn't want to tempt myself by visiting Miami.

Chapter 8

Talking to Shitara

"It's always nice to finally hear the truth"

-Neshela

Tonetta Chester

I had been home for about a week when she finally called.

"Neshela, did he call you that night?"

"No! He didn't."

"I have always wanted to know if he called you. I could never understand why he didn't call you. I know y'all was still together because I used to see the PNC deposit slips in the car with your account number. Let me tell you what happened, and maybe you can understand how I feel. J came to my house late that night. Before the suicide he told me that Charm would never see him again. He told me that he had gotten involved with some people. He said he had to meet up with them or they were going to kill his family. He said that they weren't from Newark. I tried to convince him not to go. I finally got him to go to his mother's house, but when we got there he broke down. We all cried together and begged him not to go, but he said he had to. J said that they knew where everyone lived and that they would kill us all. He explained to Nieci that he owed his boss and that he didn't know if his boss was going to let him come home. We wanted to stop him, but he walked out the door."

I interrupted. "There's no way that I would have let him walk out the door, Shitara! No way!"

"Neshela, we couldn't stop him. I felt guilty afterward, but it's not my fault. I tried to stop him. I tried."

"Shitara,—"

"Wait, listen Neshela. Before J left he gave me his wallet and watches and kissed me goodbye."

I remembered what was in his wallet. In addition to my driver's license, there was a picture of us, a picture of the whole family, and a picture of Astar and Jason together. There were no pictures of Charm. I let her keep talking.

"I broke down for the first time the other day and I decided to call you because I wanted to get this off me. Yes, I thought that you had something to do with J's death. I never really told anyone, but I know that you were his connect and I heard about your family. I put the clues together: J didn't call you that night and you didn't come to the funeral because you had something to do with it. I know you care for him because of the things we've been through, but I figure that you had no control over what had to happen. When we went to J's spot on Tifton Street to pack his things, the first thing I found on the bed was a small box and when I opened it I found a bunch of books and cards. When I opened the first book, *48 Laws of Power*, there was a note inside from you to J and your name was signed in the inside cover of the book. Everything in the box had something to do with you. There was a camera with all of your pictures from Disney World, there were recordings of y'all telling each other 'I love you.' I took this as a clue that something wasn't right with you guys. I remember when I opened J's wallet that night there were two pictures of you inside. I felt like J was trying to tell me that you had something to do with this. I didn't tell anyone at first, but I felt like it had to be you. Why wouldn't Jerri call you that night if you meant so much to him? When I first found out about you, J told me that you had a connect for him. Even when you weren't together he still kept in contact with you. I could always tell when you were back in the picture—J was extra with you. I sat on the bed worrying about my life, and all I could think was, *What did he get himself into?* I always thought you knew something. When I heard that you had a million dollar insurance policy, I really started to think. Neshela, it's been a year and we still don't know what happened to J. I just want to know what happened and if you know anything.

"Shitara, first and foremost, I'm not his connect and I had nothing to do with Jerri's death— nothing. Jerri was supposed to be here in Atlanta for his birthday so we could celebrate together. As for the insurance policy, Jerri and I set one up when I was trying to get pregnant through in-vitro. But it wasn't a million—we put $500,000 on each other just in case anything happened to us. We wanted our future kids to be taken care of. And I don't know why Jerri didn't call me the night before because we were close. We talked about everything. I talked to him the day before, but he didn't say anything out of the ordinary. He just asked me if I had money in my account and then deposited some a few hours later. Then he told me he wasn't coming to Atlanta because some business came up. Honestly, it bothered me that he didn't call me, but I know it would have bothered me more if he had and still gone through with the suicide. The way I see it, J only called people that wouldn't question his weak-ass story."

Shitara was quiet for a moment. "Raven, J's close friend, said he didn't call her either. Maybe he did only call us because he knew that we wouldn't question him. Part of me didn't believe that story, but that night I didn't know what to believe. You know how J was."

I could tell Shitara still didn't believe that I had nothing to do with J's death. "There's no way he could have told me that story. The first thing I would have asked him would have been if we had money problems. He couldn't have told me that bullshit. I don't mean to make you feel no type of way because I can't imagine your pain, and I hope you don't feel guilty because it's not your fault. He did what he wanted to do. I hate to say this, but at this point I don't know what to think."

"J gave so many signs, looking back. He told someone that he was going to Atlantic City for his birthday and if he didn't hit he was going to kill himself. Another night we was all on Central Avenue playing cards and J told Mike to order him 10 orders of wings 'cause it was his last meal. Neshela, he gave so many signs, no one read them. Everyone always had their hands out but when he needed them they weren't paying attention. I hate to admit it, but yes, I think he killed himself because nothing else makes any sense. I took my AIDS test to make sure that it wasn't the reason and it came back negative."

I began laughing.

"Why are you laughing?"

"Cause I took it twice. Who started that rumor?" I was scared as hell when I took that AIDS test.

"Monique! His so-called sister."

"Well I'm mad that J doesn't have a tombstone."

"He does, but we had to wait a year before they could lay it."

Yeah right.

I told her about calling Abdul and offering to pay for the tombstone. Most of my family was buried behind a marble wall. My uncle's funeral cost over $20,000. I had never heard of someone not having a tombstone or being buried on top of someone else. I didn't even know that shit was legal. "It's crazy that Jerri doesn't have a tombstone. Emmet, Abdul, Mike, Malik, all of them niggas, and they can't come up with $800. That's not right."

Shitara cut me off. "I don't give a fuck about none of his friends. Before J died he paid Abdul's baby mom rent for three months. You think Abdul offered that money back? J and Abdul wasn't even speaking at the time of his death. Now that J is gone, they're making money throwing parties with the theme "R.I.P. J". You would think he would check on Heaven and Charm as much as J did for him. Neshela, I don't ask them niggas for shit. As a woman I don't need any nigga to take care of my kids. It's hard but I'm going to make it. None of J's friends contributed to his tombstone—just me, his mother, brother and his two sisters. I saw Abdul a little after J died and he acted like he didn't want to speak. It blows my mind because J and he were cool too. I think they were co-defendants in a case but I'm not sure. I heard that he and J got pulled over with drugs in the car last May. Al originally took the rap for the drugs but changed his mind. I don't know what happened."

That had to be why Jerri couldn't meet me in Cancun for Memorial Day.

I asked, "Could this be what he was going to court for the week before he killed himself? "

"I don't know. I thought he was going to court for tickets. But I know he was meeting Hassan every morning." The name didn't ring a bell. "These niggas just forgot about him like he wasn't the man. When I found out that I was pregnant in November I had to let go of all the stress to be healthy for the baby. She looks just like Jerri. We named her Heaven because she is a blessing. I didn't even know I was pregnant. J left me with the gift of life! "

Shitara continued. "The other day me, Emmet and Raven was talking about you. We was mostly talking about J until Emmet brought you up. I don't know what you did to my baby's father, but he was crazy about you. I used to be talking about you like a dog and that nigga would get mad as hell. I remember when your brush was in the car and it was full of hair and I told him his girl's hair is falling out. He tried to hold it in but he couldn't help but laugh. He used to act real funny when you were in town. Emmet told us how he made you mad and you took five thousand dollars from him; I can't believe he still messed with you after that. Emmet said that J thought it was him that took it the money. That's crazy after everything he was still fucking with you. I know it was something with you, 'cause J use to fuck with a lot of girls but he didn't bring them around and definitely not around his mom and family. I know you used to leave that Ciara song on in the car, 'Pick Up the Phone.' You would always leave shit in the car because I know you wanted me to see it. One day I tried to throw your brush out the window. He almost died."

We were both laughing; I would always leave my stuff in the car because Jerri used to act like he wasn't giving her a ride to work. I knew he was. I would wait exactly 13 minutes after he walked out the door, then I would call him and say I love you just to make him say it back. I would put Ciara's song on repeat because Shitara would call over and over, so "Pick Up the Phone" was the perfect song.

The conversation went on for seven and a half hours. We laughed, we cried, we talked about everything. Jerri loved us both but for different reasons. We were different women with one thing in common: love for Jerri. I guess everybody wants a classy bitch and a ghetto bitch. After we hung up we promised to keep in contact, but I knew we wouldn't. At the end of our conversation I had more respect for this ghetto bitch.

Chapter 9

Missing Jerri

"No matter what, I will always love this man"

-Neshela

November 2, 2007

Love is a crazy thing. It seems like no matter how much you go through with that special someone, love makes you overcome so many things. I love you.

November 10, 2007

Wow J, you had me fooled. I see you was still fucking her, RAW at that you motherfucker. I guess I can only shake my head at this. I should have known. I wonder how you would have explained this to me, a baby! I wonder J, you nasty motherfucker. I hate you sometimes.

I swear, you got me questioning my position; I hate the fact that you could never be honest about her. After all, I knew you loved her. You could have had her J, but then you would have lost me. I told you a million times I wouldn't be in a love triangle with y'all. I'm not that girl Jerri!

November 13, 2007

The shit I have dealt with, fucking with your ass. I swear! I can't help but think about it Jerri. She really had your baby. You know I had to confirm it and it's true. Everyone wants to act like they don't know, but they heard it. No one came clean; I guess no one wanted to say anything. I just wonder how the hell you would have handled this. I just wonder, your ass! I swear I should have run, why did I stay?

November 22, 2007

I'm still mad but its Thanksgiving so I guess I can be nice. Astar and I had dinner at Melissa's house. It was great. Yes, Melissa! Jerri, we have become so close. You and Malik had us fooled with y'all's lying asses. We talk about you two fools all the time. I'm sure you've already heard, Malik's locked up now. Anyway, I was just thinking of you. Love ya Jerri, no matter what. See you some day.

December 2, 2007

It's almost Christmas again. I miss you so much sometimes. Astar is going to Miami for the holidays. I'll be home alone again, lonely and bored as usual. I miss you Jerri.

December 25, 2007

Merry Christmas my love!

Chapter 1o

New Years 08

"I'm looking forward to a new year and a new beginning"

-Neshela

At work, Kevin became more like my life coach than my supervisor. He was always very uplifting and positive, especially since I started coming to work in a bad mood almost every day. One day, he came over to my desk and put a book down in front of me. "You need to read this, Neshela." I looked at the front cover. *The Seat of a Soul.* I read the back cover and saw that it focused on discovering yourself through your soul. Before Jerri's death, I probably wouldn't have read a book like this, but I think death makes you more spiritual. I started reading it at my desk and stayed up the whole night to finish it. I knew this book was placed in my hands for a reason.

The next day, I went over to Kevin's desk to give him the book back, but he wasn't there. I asked the girl at the next desk where he was, and she said he was in an interview for the company director position. When he returned to his desk, I asked why he didn't tell me he was interviewing.

"Because I know I won't get the job."

"Why not?" I thought Kevin would make a great company director.

"Because they'll never hire a gay black man to run anything important around here, Neshela. I just go in for an interview every year so they can't be sued for discrimination, and every year they pass on me, making up some bullshit reason."

Hearing this made me sad. Everyone in the office knew Kevin was gay because he didn't feel the need to hide it. He didn't announce anything, but he didn't shy away from questions. I hadn't been at this job for long, but I knew Kevin was good at what he did and was very accomplished. It was unfair that the company wouldn't promote him just because he was gay. It made me dislike my job even more, but I knew I couldn't quit.

Before I knew it, Christmas came and I had no plans and no presents. Astar was in Miami—she is the most traveling child I know. I was just sitting in the house doing absolutely nothing. My job was having a Christmas party but I didn't plan to attend. I called Melissa to see if she had any plans but she didn't answer. I figured she was with her dude. She never answered when she was with him.

I called Liz and then everyone else in my phone book to wish them Happy Holidays. It was an easy way for someone with no life to waste three hours. Then I had to I think of something else to do, so I decided to have a movie night. I curled up on the couch and watched Saw I, II, and III. What a Christmas: five hours of violent movies.

The following day I was actually ready to go back to work. I had nearly died of boredom. Thirty minutes after being at work I was ready to go back home. There was nothing to do and no one was at work. I checked MySpace and Facebook. My boss sent me an email asking me to come into her office. She informed me that in October I had been late eight times. She asked me to sign a paper saying that I could not be late again for three months or I would be terminated. The bitch had better be glad I needed this job because I was ready to rip this paper up and throw it in her face.

In October, I had not wanted to wake up on many mornings. I just signed the form because I knew I didn't have an attendance problem. Shit, I didn't have anything to do but work; she was probably just looking for a way to fire me.

Right after I signed the form, she said in her squeaky white girl voice, "Oh I remember I think your boyfriend got killed or something. Like a year ago!" I could have jumped across the desk and beat her with the nearby phone. I had to get away from her before I lost my job.

I left work at 5:00 o'clock on the dot—fuck staying late or coming in early. I'll be here on time and I'll leave on time every day, or otherwise Corporate America will fire your ass. But I was only going to do the bare minimum to keep this job. Over the next few weeks I went from enjoying my job to just doing it.

New Year's Eve came and I didn't even have the energy to get up and go to church. The year 2008 was supposed to be a new beginning. I could use one. I had been thinking about going to see a psychologist. My aunt had suggested grief therapy some time ago. I hadn't put any thought into it at the time, but now I was thinking I could use it.

I spent way too much time thinking about Jerri and comparing every dude I met to him. I didn't think it was that obvious until one dude told me that he was tired of competing with my dead boyfriend. I was so sick of eating at Cheesecake Factory, acting like I was at a five-star restaurant. When we finally went to a real restaurant this nigga didn't even know the salad fork from the dinner fork. I tell you, higher education doesn't mean shit, because he had a PhD and no table manners.

I finally went to see a psychologist. I didn't know if I was depressed or lonely, but I knew something was wrong. This was one of the most difficult decisions that I had ever made in my life. Considering my major was psychology in school, I knew the position of the doctor—analyze and assess. I wasn't sure that I was ready to be analyzed by anyone but God, but I made my decision anyway.

There were over eighty psychologists in Alpharetta. Then I remembered that there was a large upper middle class, and a large portion of them were soccer moms.

I made an appointment with the first doctor on the list. He was a white male, and I felt like I was wasting my time because he seemed like he couldn't relate to what I was going through. He was considerate, but when I was telling him all the details, he looked at me like I was speaking another language. He also acted as if he had never seen a black person before. After an hour he suggested that I come back in two weeks. I nodded in agreement but didn't reschedule.

The next day I made an appointment with an older Indian psychiatrist whose office was right next to my house. But after an hour with her, I felt crazy. This woman gave me three prescriptions: one for depression, one for sleeping and another that I had no clue what it was for. I had no plans to see her again. I might have been a little depressed and had problems sleeping, but I'd be damned if I was going to take pills.

The following day I talked to my aunt and mom. My aunt said that I needed someone to talk to. My mother told me I needed to pray. She swore that prayer was the answer to everything. She used to curse like a sailor and have a glass of Alize every night. Now she prays instead of curses, and her Alize is now grape juice.

After a few days of reasoning with myself, I gave it one more shot. I wrote down the names of five more doctors, put their names into a bowl, and picked one. Richard Gerry. I hoped that he was the one, because if he wasn't, I was done with this therapy thing.

After taking my personal information, Dr. Gerry's receptionist said that he was only available in a week. I decided to make the appointment anyway. Before I could hang up, she asked, "Are you from Miami?" She must have recognized the 305 area code.

"I'm from Ft. Lauderdale," she said. "I miss the beach so much sometimes." She went on for a few minutes about beautiful South Florida, and it made me homesick.

A week later I arrived for my appointment. Within a few minutes a young man came to the door and called my name. I was surprised to see that he was black. As we entered his office, I instantly felt welcome and like I could open up to him before I even sat on the couch. The room was decorated in warm earth tones that made the room very inviting. He dimmed the lights and asked if I wanted some water. "No thanks," I said. "I hate water!" He grinned as he closed the door and sat in an oversized chair. I plopped into a chair across from him and poured my heart out. For the first time, I felt that someone was really listening to me. I don't know if it was just because he was African-American, but it felt more like two friends talking than a psychologist and a patient. I made an appointment to come back the following Thursday at 6:00pm.

Chapter 11

Green Eyes

Green: The hue of that portion of the visible spectrum lying

between yellow and blue.

Eyes: An organ of vision or of light sensitivity

I was watching Oprah when I received an email on my MySpace page. *"I would like to talk to u about J. My name is Green Eyes, I don't know if J ever talked about me but I was his dude. I was locked up at the time all this was going on. U can ask Quan, Mack, Wesley, or Abdul about me, they'll let u know. Even Mimi can cosign since that's your girl. If at all possible, please get back at me. —Green Eyes."*

I never heard of him and I don't need anyone to check him out.

"Why do I need to validate you? You said my man's name and that's good enough for me. What do you want? You can send your question just like you sent this message. —Neshela."

"I have a few questions that it seems no one is willing to answer. I have been trying to find shit out; Abdul is the only one I can depend on. Emmet is on some other shit now; we had this falling out over J not having a tombstone. This is being taken care of. I spoke to Abdul about u. He told me that my dude loved u and I probably can get some answers from u. The funny part about all of this is I have even heard about u, but nobody seems to want to talk about u and I was wondering why? Anyway I hope to talk to u soon." At the end of the message he left his phone number.

I dialed his number but then I quickly hung up because I forgot to press *67 to block my number. It was too late. My phone was ringing back and it was his number on my screen.

"Somebody just call GE?"

"This is Neshela. Do you have a real name?"

"Hassan. I'm just wondering if you know what happened to my dude."

Was he trying to be funny? "I wish I did but I don't. What made you get at me?"

"Shitara told me about you. We have been trying to figure this whole thing out. She mentioned you a few times so I just took it upon myself to see if you know anything."

"I don't know anything. You may want to call the chick he called 'cause he didn't call me that night. And about the tombstone, you niggas finally decided to get him one! Shitara told me that she ordered it last year, but I know that was a lie because when I went to see him he still didn't have one. Thank God somebody's doing something...it's only been a year and a half!"

"Yeah, thanks to you! I heard that slick shit you said about Alpine, and you're right, my nigga should have been buried the proper way. There's no need to cry over spilled milk. Like you, I heard that bullshit for a while, but he is really getting one now and that's my word. You'll have something to see the next time that you are here."

"Your word?" His word didn't mean shit to me.

"Yeah, my word, ma'am. I'll keep you posted on everything with regards to the tombstone. I can call you at this number, right?"

"Yeah this is my number. Call me when they lay the tombstone."

After I hung up the phone, I checked out Mr. Green Eyes' profile on MySpace. He was kind of cute, but there was something spooky-looking about his eyes. I quickly minimized his MySpace page because his eyes were killing me. Then I called him back and hammered him with questions. We were on the phone for two hours. He ended our conversation when he pulled up to the skating rink on Route 22. He said he would call me back after he was done skating. Over the next few days I had one continuous chat with Mr. Green Eyes about J.

We always started with small talk about the tombstone. He never talked about himself. At this point I was trying to figure out his motive. I didn't understand him, but I played it cool and just listened to everything he said. By Friday I knew all that I needed to know.

My ears itched to learn more, about everyone and everything still in NJ—he seemed to be the closest contact to J's baby mom and his family. As we sat on the phone, for the fifth day straight, I moved to get into a better position to hear the story about his relationship with Jerri.

"Damn!" I shout.

"You okay?"

"I just popped my necklace, listening to your crazy ass!"

"Can you fix it?"

"I think I'll just get another one. It's just a thin box necklace that's only two or three hundred dollars." Later he said that he would be flying to Atlanta next Friday for a party. He asked if he could take me to dinner. I simply asked him what he thought Jerri would say. "J is dead, but life goes on. I'm sure he wanted you to enjoy your life. Besides, I just want to take you dinner. It would be nice to meet you since I'll be in Atlanta. "

I told him to call me when he got there.

I had to call my mother about this one. Jackie had the best game in the world. I needed a crash course in disloyal disrespectful-ass niggas. This was all new for me. I called my mother and told her about Green Eyes.

She spent fifteen minutes running down the game on disloyal niggas. At the end of her lecture she said, "Everything happens for a reason, baby. Be careful, you don't know his intentions. He may be working with them people. He may think you know something or he might just be trying to screw you. Nevertheless, he could be the love of your life. Who knows, let him keep doing all the talking. Don't tell him anything important and don't talk about family business."

She was talking to me like I was four years old.

"I'm just reminding you," she said. "You know I liked J."

I knew my mother—she hadn't liked Jerri at all. But he used to play the lottery for her and call her to check up on me when I wasn't taking his calls, so I knew they talked.

"I did like J, I just didn't like him for you. He was a sweet guy, Neshela. I just never wanted you to have to go through losing a spouse and everything else that comes with being with a hustler wife. I never believed that he committed suicide. That just didn't seem like him, not to me! At least not the J I knew. Neshela, there are still questions that are unanswered. Just be careful."

I thought I had closed this chapter in my life. I sat on the couch missing him. Then Hassan called to give me an update about Jerri's tombstone, saying that everything was paid for and the tombstone would arrive in a few weeks. I sighed with relief, confident that it was going to get done. While chatting with Hassan, I lost track of time.

The conversation with Hassan was getting interesting. He was telling me about his crew and how he got involved in the first place.

He ended our conversation by saying, "So do you think J really loved you? You know he had a lot of girls!"

"I don't know too many niggas that will pay 6 G's for a bitch to get pregnant, so what do you think?" I hung up the phone and went to get some groceries for dinner. The traffic was light. A white eighteen wheeler blocked my view, and I saw the word Alpine on the side of the truck in big bold letters. The slogan read "Where We Always Put You First." My heart dropped. Was this just a coincidence or was it a sign? Then my cell phone rang. It was Hassan again.

Chapter 12

Getaway

"I remember when I used to go to Jersey just to get away.......
The old days"

-Neshela

This weekend Quan and Mimi were flying in for a weekend getaway. I had the whole weekend planned. It was like the old days when I used to fly to Jersey. But now the tables were turned; Quan and Mimi were in Atlanta. We planned to chill and watch movies.

After the usual spa visit and shopping, we had our last supper at P.F. Chang's on Sunday night. Mimi asked what was for dessert. I wondered how she kept her figure. We ordered banana rolls and ice cream. Finally, the fortune cookies arrived. We read our fortunes aloud. Mine was, "The love of your life will appear in front of you unexpectedly." We laughed. At that moment Hassan called to see how I was doing. After dinner we went to see Tyler Perry's *Meet the Browns.*

On Monday morning I woke up 20 minutes late but I still cooked T-bone steak and eggs. We had to eat fast to make it to the airport on time. The traffic on 400 was crazy and I remembered why I don't go anywhere before 10:00 am. We barely made it.

After Quan and Mimi left, Hassan and I went back to our regular talks. I had wanted to ask Mimi and Quan about Hassan but didn't. I kept Hassan a secret. At some point it would all come out.

On Friday, the funniest thing happened. Hassan called to tell me that his friends missed their flight to Atlanta and he was wondering if we could do breakfast, lunch and dinner. This is my type of nigga; I love free meals, but I couldn't act beat. I figured that he had a hidden agenda. His boys were probably never coming in the first place. I said that I would be available for dinner.

On the day of the dinner, I dragged Melissa along. I met her at the restaurant and I gave her the rundown about Green Eyes. The plan was for her to be at the restaurant when we arrived. Her job was to pay attention. I was not into being played.

I went to the LaQuinta Inn to pick up Hassan. Who the hell stays at the LaQuinta? It's in Dunwoody, which is a wonderful area, but it's still the LaQuinta! I saw him walking toward me. He was gorgeous, but the first thing I noticed were that his eyes didn't look green at all, but were clear like water. He stood over 6 feet tall and had a sexy muscular build. His dreads fell past his shoulders, but it was his eyes that had me mesmerized. He was wearing a white polo, dark denim jeans, and a pair of fresh Forces. I wanted to bite my bottom lip, but I couldn't show any emotion. Instead, I extended my hand to greet him. "Hello Mr. Anonymous. I'm Neshela!"

"It's nice to put a face to the voice." He looked shocked, as if he was expecting me to be ugly and fat. "You are simply gorgeous!"

"Thank you." He had a perfect smile. He reminded me of somebody. At this point I forgot all about the cheap-ass hotel or the fact that he might be broke.

"We're having dinner at Fleming's Prime Steakhouse. It's one of my favorite spots. I hope you like it." He didn't reply. He seemed a little shy, but he talked a lot over the phone so I was puzzled.

"What are you thinking about?"

His reply shocked the hell out of me. "You, why do you ask?" he said. Now I was sitting quietly, just hoping this nigga wasn't trying to get at me. He looks good as hell but he's still my man's dude and I don't get down like that.

We arrive at the Fleming. The hostess greets us at the door. "Ms. Jones, I can seat you right away." She already knew what table I wanted. Over dinner we talk about ourselves, not about J. I look directly in his eyes and ask, "How do you think Jerri would feel about you taking me to dinner?"

"I don't think he'd care." Jerri was jealous as hell. He was probably rolling over in his grave. I changed the subject because I didn't want to get mad and because my steak was too good not to enjoy. As we got up to leave after the meal, I looked across the restaurant to Melissa and gave her a wink, letting her know that everything was okay.

After dinner, I drove him back to his hotel. I texted his room number to Melissa in case I came up missing. As we walked into his room he asked me where we could hang out for the night. "I see you have plans for me, now we're hanging out too!" He laughed and walked across the room to retrieve a little green jewelry box. I opened it and inside was a thin box necklace just like the one I had broken. A second later he handed me a piece of paper. It was a sketched copy of Jerri's tombstone. I sat on the edge of the bed and looked at the paper over and over again. I thanked him, wanting to cry, and he smiled.

We hung out at Lucky Lounge that night and he stayed on my ass the whole night. After the club I dropped him to his hotel and went home. I woke up Saturday morning staring at the picture of J and me, reminiscing. I'll never forget that day—we were at a birthday party that my girlfriend Kay was throwing for her daughter. It was a few days before Shitara called to tell me that I ruined her happy home, the one I had no idea about. The picture was taken during the happy days when I was still pregnant with the twins. Putting the picture down, I brushed my teeth and crawled back into bed.

A few hours later, my phone rang. It was Melissa calling to tell me that all her tires were flat. Her boyfriend had just proposed, and when his baby mom found out, she went to work on Melissa's car. I would have been pissed too, but right now this whole thing was amusing. Melissa hung up on me because I was laughing so hard, but I stopped and called her back to make sure she was good.

Green Eyes then called to ask if we could have dinner at the Olive Garden, his favorite restaurant. I couldn't believe what I was hearing. Who the hell eats at Olive Garden?

I got dressed. His hotel wasn't that far from me. If he had come to Atlanta to party, why was he staying in the suburbs? I made it to his hotel in 15 minutes, but before he came downstairs I quickly cleaned up my car. I scooped up everything that had my home address on it and threw it in the glove box. Then I dialed his number. "Hassan, I'm downstairs. Can you ask someone at the front desk how to get to Olive Garden? I have no clue where it is."

Olive Garden was right around the corner on Ashford-Dunwoody next to J Alexander, a real restaurant. The hostess sat us in a small booth in the corner. I was starving. I ordered spaghetti with a coat of cheese baked over the top and he ordered seafood Alfredo. The food took a while to arrive. After dinner we drove to the city because I wanted peach cobbler from Rare, a tapas restaurant I have always liked. Dining at Rare was always an experience, and their peach cobbler was delicious. "Do you have a reservation?" the hostess asked. I said that we just wanted to sit at the bar. I ordered my peach cobbler and Hassan ordered a double shot of Patron. As we left, the sky began to cry. Thank God I was wearing a hood; I couldn't afford for my hair to get wet. It took the valet just a few minutes to pull up my car and off we went.

By the time we made it to Hassan's hotel it was pouring. He invited me up. I accepted and parked my car. We entered the elevator as the doors began to close. He pressed number five and smiled. Within seconds, we were outside of his hotel room, 528.

We woke up the next morning to the chirping of his Nextel. A squeaky voice came across the phone and was saying Green Eyes' name. Her voice sounded familiar.

Hassan sleepily picked up the phone. "What's up?"

"We're having a party for Charm next weekend. Don't forget to come by the park."

It was Shitara! He said okay and rolled back over. What the fuck I was doing? I was completely dressed with all of my clothes from the night before and so was he, but he was holding me close as hell. I slept the night away with Mr. Green Eyes.

Chapter 13

With All Due Respect

Respect: To feel or show deferential regard for; esteem.

I couldn't wait to see my therapist again. It had been a long week. I needed an hour session to get this shit off my chest. Jerri O. Hopkins' tombstone was finally going to be laid. I was so happy that the day had come, even if it was a year late. Hassan emailed me the picture of Jerri's tombstone. I cried so hard. But I noticed a few things, like how at the bottom of the tombstone there were a lot of initials crowded together. I had never seen that before on any tombstone. I thought I was reading an obituary with all of the people he left behind. I didn't remember it being this way when Hassan showed me the sketch a month ago. I pulled out the drawing and saw that it was indeed the same. These unintelligent motherfuckers, just when I thought I'd seen it all!

I called Liz and Melissa to share the news. When I read them the writing on the tombstone they were silent. I knew what they were thinking, so I said, "With all due respect to the dead and the man I love, this is some crazy shit!" Melissa went first. "Neshela, I haven't got past the first line. Read that dumb shit again! See what you was messing with?"

"You damn black American," Liz said in her Jamaican accent.

I had to defend their stupid. "Y'all crazy. We can see that they're not used to buying tombstones so they didn't know what was supposed to go on them." I laughed.

Melissa started in again. "Make all the excuses you want for your man and this friends Nobody didn't think to walk around the graveyard and read to see what's supposed to go on tombstones."

"Okay, you win."

After I hung up the phone, I got dressed to see my psychologist. I told him all about it; he just looked at me like, *What the hell is that?* Then he reminded me that I always expect people to do what I think is right. "Sometimes people just don't know any better." I guess that was obvious.

After therapy I took myself to dinner at my new favorite spot, Seasons 52. Tommy had taken me on a dinner date at Seasons 52 awhile back, and I'd been going ever since. The filet mignon is excellent; it's only 6 oz but it's filling. The grilled carrots and garlic mashed potatoes are so good too. After dinner I took the long way home. I had already paid the babysitter for three hours so I still had some time.

When I got home Astar was sound asleep. Our babysitter, Megan, was watching BET and talking on the phone. I walked her down the hill and saw her into her house. I jumped in the shower and brushed my teeth. I thought of Jerri and Hassan—I can't think of them separately. I had thought that Jerri was the love of my life. Now I was dating his friend. I pulled my handheld shower head from its mount, changed the setting to a higher pressure and placed it on my clit. I remember when Jerri showed me this technique. He placed our gold shower head on my clit and moved it back and forth.

I couldn't stop thinking about the love we used to make. I wished Jerri was here, by my side. Waking up wasn't the same without him. I wondered how life would be if he was here. I knew we wouldn't still be together, not after Heaven. I still loved him.

Sometimes I felt him right next to me. I was still trying to find a way to get through this. I wanted him so bad sometimes, but I was trying to come to the realization that Jerri had been too good for this earth. He had another life now, and I understood why God wanted him on his side. But every now and then I wished he could just come by and hug me.

My therapist said that my depression was getting better and that I was working through the grief. I was finally getting a full night's sleep. He also said that writing to Jerri was a good form of therapy. He suggested that I take some vitamins; my eating habits are still horrible even though I cook dinner every night. I rarely eat, and I actually need to lose fifteen pounds. I called Quan to ask about some diet pills. Quan lives in the gym, so he would know. It's crazy—I won't take pills for anything except to lose weight.

A few days later he sent me a list of shit to do to get in shape and lose weight. There was a small box of pills. Quan told me that one of the vitamins would make me fertile, so he suggested that I be careful. I was not fucking shit, and the bullet or shower head couldn't get me pregnant.

With my new cheat sheet and diet pills, I got ready for the gym. I was committed to getting in shape. For the first few days it was easy, but after a week, I was done. My lazy ass wasn't cut out for this gym shit. I continued taking the vitamins, but the gym days were over.

I had been on vacation for a week and was so not ready to go back to work. My job was interesting; I could just sit at my desk and watch the down low guys pass by. Kevin was the one who warned me about who was down low and who wasn't because I honestly couldn't tell. These dudes would always be at my desk trying to find out if I was single, but Kevin would just shake his head, which meant stay away and keep moving. I wasn't really feeling them anyway. I respected gay men who were open but not men who fuck other men and pretend that they are straight. I vowed not to fuck anything in Atlanta. This job was a true eye opener; I left work every day at 5:00 pm sharp. I didn't love my job, but the money was good.

I usually got home at 5:40 pm; I made dinner and then relaxed. Astar went to Miami for her summer break. Lately after dinner I would get on the phone with Hassan. He put me to sleep just about every night and called every morning at 7:50, and we talked while he took his daughter to school. It was crazy how much we talked. He was going to be in town for a day, and after seeing a play on Saturday we were having dinner at Fleming's Steakhouse.

At dinner, he kissed me for the first time. It was a little odd, but nice. He simply gave me a kiss on my forehead to thank me for a lovely weekend. Hassan took an early flight out of Atlanta on Sunday morning. After spending the weekend with Hassan, I had to prepare myself for work. My job didn't require much, but it was just the fact that I had to go to work at all. It was also my birthday; I was 27. I couldn't believe I was going to work on my birthday. I told Kevin about my birthday the week before and he surprised me with flowers and a card. I swear he treated me better than the straight guys I had dated!

I wasn't expecting anything from anyone else. A few of my homeboys sent some flowers and when I finally got a chance to check my voicemail Rachel, Melissa and Mimi all left their birthday wishes. Astar sang "Happy Birthday" in Spanish on my voicemail. I couldn't understand a single word, but she sounded so cute. She was still in Miami, and hearing her voice made me miss her even more. After a long day of work I headed home to relax.

It was about 6:40 pm when Hassan called from the Atlanta airport. He said that he was going to take a cab to The Westin and that I should meet him there. *I'm surprised that he's back ten days early... he just left yesterday.* I like surprises, though. When I arrived at the hotel, Hassan had already checked in. I went directly to his room. He opened the door holding a dozen long-stemmed white roses with a birthday card. How did he know that white roses were my favorite? Jerri used to get them for me whenever I came home. I wished Hassan had picked another color. But I was really starting to like him! He only stayed for a day, but it was one of the best days I had had in a long time.

Chapter 14

Summertime

"Most people enjoy the summer, but fall is my favorite time of year"

-Neshela

It's hot in "Hotlanta." Gay dudes are everywhere and most of them look good. I never understood why anyone would want to be gay until I met Mike, Tamika's friend. He's crazy as hell and we call him "sexy black." One day over lunch, Mike explained to me why men were gay. He believed he was born gay, and from the way he was describing it, he felt he was trapped in the wrong body. He said for a long time he tried to ignore it and be in heterosexual relationships and even had children. "It just became too difficult to live a life I wasn't comfortable with," he said. "But Atlanta changed all that for me. It's the black San Francisco!" I didn't care what people's sexual preferences were, even when I didn't understand them. Maybe I wasn't supposed to. As long as he was happy, I was happy for him.

Since Astar was spending the summer with her pappy, I took advantage of the break. Melissa and I went out every chance we got and that night Puffy was having a party at Justin's and Melissa was invited. I didn't ask any questions when she called with the news. This would be our first trip back to Justin's after walking out on a $200 check earlier this year. It was Melissa's idea; she can be an asshole and I guess I was game. Everyone else was leaving anyway.

Melissa said we had two hours to get dressed, but I planned to be ready in 45 minutes; I was ready to party. We arrived at Justin's just in time for the grand celebration. Puffy was announcing his new line of perfume. I scanned the room to see if I knew anyone. Jay headed toward me. I hadn't seen him in years. I knew him because he was an R&B singer who was signed to my uncle's label. We played catch up and exchanged contact information. The evening was going great. Melissa and I were having a ball. I collected a few more business cards and left after two hours.

Melissa and I even went to Puerto Rico and then New York City. I always set a goal to take three vacations and one international trip a year. Melissa and I had covered two—I just needed one more place to go. Since I had a week off, I was going to book a ticket to Vegas and Miami to see Astar.

After I booked my ticket the phone rang. It was Albie. He had just found out that his son had joined a gang. I felt so bad for him because Albie was a good person. We talked all night. Albie and his ex-wife had been divorced for more than ten years and he thought that the bad relationship between the two of them was the reason why his son was so distant. I could hear the hurt in his voice. As our conversation came to a close, Albie said that he had to separate himself from his son. He called it "tough love." I didn't agree but didn't argue. He just needed someone to listen. Albie and I had debated about his son a few times already. He thought I was soft and I thought he was too strict. But I knew this whole thing was hard for him so I was not going to say much. Besides, I had a flight to Vegas in the morning. Then I was flying to Miami for a few days to see my baby.

I didn't hang up with Albie until after midnight. I knew that the time difference in Vegas was going to kill me. When the flight landed at Las Vegas airport five hours later, I had the worst jet lag ever. I took a car service to the Bellagio where I would be for the next four days. This trip would be all about me; I would see a few shows and shop a little. This was my first trip to Las Vegas. Jerri and I were supposed to meet everyone in Vegas to see the Mayweather fight. I'll never forget November 4, 2006, because instead of being in Vegas, I was at home crying and Jerri had been buried. I guess that was why I took this trip.

I rested for most of the day. I refused to go outside because it was 114 degrees. I didn't know it could get this hot. I really didn't understand how people lived here. At 7:00 p.m. the sun was still shining. I walked around the casino, but gambling had never been my thing, so I headed back to my room to wait for the sun to set. At 8:30 the sun finally went down. I got dressed and headed to the Eiffel Tower at the Paris hotel. I couldn't wait to see the water show. Although I could see it from my room, I heard that it was extra beautiful from the Eiffel Tower.

I made it just in time. "My Heart Will Go On" by Celine Dion had just begun as I exited the elevator. I was at the very top of the Eiffel Tower and the view was amazing. As I watched the water bounce back and forth to the rhythm of the song, I couldn't help but think of Jerri at the same time. Tears began to flow. The lyrics won't allow me to stop thinking of my lost love. Sometimes just the thought of not having him hurt.

The next morning I went to the Forum shop at Caesar's Palace. It was time to treat myself to Gucci, La Perla and Christian Dior. I hadn't been to La Perla in about a year. I couldn't afford to waste $300 on panties, but I was going to make an exception. After I left Caesar's Palace I headed over to the fashion show at the mall. Vegas was a woman's paradise, at least for me.

After three long, hot days in Las Vegas it was time to go to Miami. I enjoyed Vegas; it was something about being there that made me feel like Jerri was with me. On the way to the airport I called Hassan. Then I called Liz to give her the details on my flight. My flight would land at Ft. Lauderdale International Airport at 11:50 p.m. Liz would pick me up and we'd go straight to this new spot in South Beach called The Fifth's. I was hoping to enjoy myself, but I also couldn't wait to see my daughter.

After a long night of partying I realized that Miami was still the same. The following day I went to see my baby. I took her to our favorite Cuban restaurant for lunch. A few hours later I flew to

Atlanta and made it home in time to watch a rerun of "The Wire" on BET.

A few minutes into the show the house phone rang. Hardly anyone had my home phone number. It was Melissa.

I couldn't make out what she was saying. She was screaming and crying at the same time. Finally I coaxed the story out of her. Her fiancé was missing and his car had been found on the side of the road near their home. I remembered the day that Mimi called to tell me about Jerri.

I asked her for Ron's full name and date of birth. I told her to call the lawyer and leave a message. I called all the local jails and hospitals. After two hours, I couldn't find anything. I hated to call Melissa but I had to. I truly understood her pain. I gave her the news but told her to stay positive. The Feds can hold someone for up to 72 hours before releasing any information. I invited her to my spot for a few days so she wouldn't be alone.

The very next day the attorney called to tell us that the Feds in North Carolina had indicted Ronald on money laundering charges. The lawyer said that he had a bond for $500,000. That wasn't much for the Feds. Melissa gathered all the documents that the lawyer requested and that evening we drove to Greenville, North Carolina to pick Ronald up. It seemed like the longest road trip ever.

On the way back I talked to Hassan. Since my Vegas trip I'd been distant, but I missed talking to Hassan. I really liked him, but it was just something about Vegas.

The summer ended and I prepared myself to be a mommy again. Astar would be coming home over the weekend. I missed my baby; I talked to her every day but it was not at all like having her home. It's funny how I missed my kid until she came back.

I was at the airport two hours early. When she got off the plane she ran into my arms. I took her to have ice cream. Then we went to the mall to pick up a few Webkins. We used the evening to catch up. We got home just in time to watch "That's So Raven," Astar's favorite show.

Chapter 15

Lost

"You can't control who you fall in love with"

-Neshela

After the first weekend with Hassan I was lost. I didn't know what to do. Now it had been four months and I couldn't go a day without talking to him. He'd been in Atlanta a lot I was falling for him. I didn't know what I was doing, but I was enjoying every minute of it. Hassan's flight would land at 2:42 pm, and I couldn't wait to see him.

I still hadn't told anyone about Hassan. It was too dangerous and I didn't need anyone from Jersey asking me questions. But I was just dying to tell someone about him. I decided to tell Kevin. He always told me about his husband or partner or whatever he called him, so I figured I could tell him about Hassan. After I told him all of the details, he sighed and gave me a disapproving look.

"Neshela, what the hell are you doing?"

"What do you mean what am I doing?"

"Neshela, you ran away from that detective who wanted to do you in for Jerri's murder." I forgot I had told him about everything that happened in Newark, and he knew who Jerri was because I had his pictures on my desk. "It's bad enough that you talked to that police officer for so long on the phone, but now you have this guy that's suddenly trying to get with you, saying he knows Jerri? That's messed up."

I just had to laugh. "Boy, you stupid! Hassan was in jail when Jerri was killed, so that's why he's talking to me now. And he didn't try to get with me at first. He's not like that."

"I'm just saying, Neshela. Watch out. What are you doing with your dead man's dude anyway? I would just lay low until the whole thing in Newark blows over for good."

"Whatever." I was mad at Kevin for thinking that Hassan was trying to play me, and worse, that I could even be played.

I sat at my desk for a while thinking about what Kevin said. Was he being paranoid, or was I just too charmed by Hassan? From the bare facts I told him, it probably looked sketchy. I wanted to tell Mimi so bad, but I didn't want her reacting the same way Kevin did. I was enjoying my time with Hassan, and I wasn't going to let anyone make me feel bad about it.

I left work three hours early to pick him up from the airport. We hugged as usual but we had lust in our eyes. Part of me wanted to give in to him, but I couldn't; we had become good friends.

Once we collected Hassan's bags from baggage claim we went to Season 52 for dinner. Hassan hated this restaurant but it was my favorite and I was being selfish. I enjoyed dinner, but he didn't. After dinner we checked in at the Westin. I chilled with him for most of the evening. We just watched TV and made small talk until we both fell asleep.

I woke up at 4:30 and left quietly. I had to be home before Astar woke up. Megan was staying for the weekend, but I liked to be home to say good morning to my baby. I got home at 5:00, jumped in the shower, brushed my teeth and slipped into my PJ's. A few hours later, Astar came to my room to say good morning. I bounced out of bed to cook breakfast for the girls, picked up my mail, and went to see Green Eyes.

As Hassan got into the car I noticed my mail on the seat. He picked up the mail, glanced at it and then handed it to me. I wished it was a bill, so that I could hand it back to him, but it wasn't. I just hope he wasn't paying attention to my address, but with his eyes and blank expression I couldn't tell.

We had breakfast at the Original Pancake House, another one of my favorite spots. As I was sitting across the table looking at him, it finally dawned on me. He looked just like Gary Dourdan from the Janet Jackson video "Again" with a dash of AJ Calloway from 106 & Park. He had Gary's green eyes and AJ's long dreads. He was just as sexy as the first time I saw him. After breakfast we headed to the movies and then we went back to his room.

We sat on the bed chatting; there was something about this dude that made me laugh. I was happy when I was with him. I had no intention of liking him, but I did and wanted more. I looked into his eyes, and he was looking into mine. I was watching his lips move but I couldn't hear him and I think he knew that I was lusting for him. His lips began touching mine. I couldn't resist him. I was saying no in my mind but my heart was convinced that this was what I wanted. For some reason, the word no wouldn't come out. He had me hypnotized. My body was doing everything that he wanted. He was kissing me all over, not missing a spot. He pushed my legs apart and began to taste me. I couldn't believe I was letting this happen.

Bow Wow and Ciara came through the radio singing "Like You," mine and Jerri's song. I couldn't help but think of him. I felt the tears coming to my eyes. But I couldn't stop him; the pleasure of his lips on my clit wouldn't allow me to. I haven't been with a man in forever. I let my mind play games as I began to think of Jerri with other women, cheating on me. I was using anything I could as an excuse to enjoy this moment. It had been over twenty minutes and he hadn't come up for air. It felt so good my legs wouldn't stop shaking. I felt him entering me, and I exhaled. My legs were wide open I could feel every thrust back and forth. Without exiting, he turned my body to the side and maintained the rhythm...I was pushing back, and I noticed that he was loving it, so I began to push harder. I watched him bite his bottom lip; he was feeling it and so was I. I was pushing hard. I wanted him to come first, but he placed his hand on my waist to gain control of my movement. The room was spinning and I could barely breathe. I was trying to hold back—I wanted to win this one. I was going to take him for all he's got. He pulled me closer as he began to move more forcefully. His silent breathing became aggressive; he was about to come and I knew it. He placed both of his hands on my waist, trying to gain control again. I let him have his way. I just lay there and began to squeeze my pussy muscles; I was smiling because I knew I got him.

I couldn't believe this had just happened. It all began with a kiss. As I lay in the bed next to him, totally exhausted, I noticed a cross tattooed on his arm that read R.I.P. J. I closed my eyes trying so hard not to think of it, but even with my eyes closed, I couldn't stop the tears. He pulled me close and kissed my forehead, and in my ear he whispered, "Neshela I'm not going anywhere, I promise. I'm down for you but I hate it when you get so emotional about him." He looked directly into my eyes. I just looked back at him. I was still in shock. Was he jealous of my feelings for Jerri?

I guess he had to prove himself. Before I realized it I was on my hands and knees and he was fucking the shit out of me. A man's pride is a funny thing. In the shower, he washed my back, and I washed his. I still couldn't help thinking of Jerri.

When Hassan looked at me and kissed my lips, all those thoughts went away. I was making new memories, with a new man. We then set off for Olive Garden. I was starting to like Olive Garden. I ordered spaghetti which was great as usual. I always enjoyed my time with Hassan. After dinner we went to the Margaret Mitchell House Museum to attend my friend Kole Black's book release. He was finally releasing *The Chances She Took*, a novel that I had been dying to read. Kole wouldn't let me read an advance copy because he wanted me to attend the big affair tonight.

We were having so much fun, but It was midnight and the weekend was ending. Hassan always left on Sunday evenings. I already missed him and he wasn't even gone yet. I wasn't sure how I would make it through the next two weeks. We returned to Hassan's room to get a few hours of rest. It had been a long day; we lay in the bed staring into each other's eyes until we both fell asleep.

The ringing of my cell phone woke me. It was Mimi. Something was wrong. I went into the bathroom where I listened to her cry. Someone had died, so she cried and I listened. Twenty minutes later, she said that she would call me back. I didn't ask any questions.

Hassan was still asleep, so I took a shower. When I came out, Hassan was sitting up in bed with his cell phone against his ear and saying, "That's crazy." After hanging up, he told me that Jack, one of the NJ Boys, found out that his girlfriend had been kidnapped and murdered. I suspected that was the person that Mimi had been talking about; she and Jack's girlfriend had been good friends.

As Hassan and I went to the airport we talked about the tragedy. Afterwards I called Mimi and reminded her to be careful.

Chapter 16

Rob's Home

"Freedom Is a blessing. Damn I missed my family"

-Rob

I flew home for my brother's release from prison. I hadn't seen him in five years. Even though I had visited people in prison, I could never get used to the feeling of being there. I have always told my dude if he went to prison for more than five years, our relationship was over.

The celebration was wonderful; I spent most of the evening trying to talk my brother into moving to Atlanta. He didn't seem interested. I would love to have my brother and his children in the same city as me. I wanted him to see that there was more to life than the streets. I hoped Rob had reached that point. He had to live for God, his children and his wife.

Coming to Miami hadn't been a bad idea after all. It was nice to see all of my family together for something that wasn't a funeral or a trial. I was so proud of the new generation: two of my little cousins were finishing up law school, one was in medical school, and another cousin had just graduated with honors from the University of Miami. Our family had come so far.

We had the evening planned: dinner at Benihana, my brother's favorite restaurant, then Trick's album release party at Club Mansion. That was what we had told my brother, at least. We were really having a welcome home party. I was looking forward to the club; this was the first time that I had partied with my family. Partying with them was different from partying with Melissa. My uncle pulled out all the big boy cars: the GT, Lambo, Rolls Royce. Since it was Rob's welcome home party, it was guaranteed to be a star-studded event. Uncle Bert even invited all his ballplayer friends.

I was all dressed and waiting for Uncle Bert to drop off his Maserati so that I could head to the club. I liked to show up late and leave early, but Bert was taking forever. I guess I was excited; the Maserati was my favorite car. I couldn't wait to get my own. As my uncle pulled up, Liz called to tell me that she had just arrived at the club and that is was crazy. Banners all over the place read "Welcome Home Little One," which was my brother's nickname.

When I finally pulled up to the club it was about 1:15 a.m. People were everywhere. As I walked through the doors, Tony, one of the managers, pulled my arm. He put three bands on my wrist because the bouncers were going be firm tonight. I saw so many familiar faces but I didn't waste time speaking to them. I was trying to find my brother and my cell phone wasn't getting a signal; Mansion is one of the biggest clubs on South Beach. I was heading upstairs. Still no luck. Little did I know these fools were on the stage. My brother appeared to be having a ball. Everyone was so happy to have him back home; it had only been five years, but it seemed like a lifetime.

I was having a ball when the alarm on my cell phone went off. I only had fifteen minutes left to party. I don't spend more than two hours in a club. It was just my way of keeping my face fresh. It seemed like time was flying by and I was having so much fun, but I had to call it a night and get the hell out of there.

I headed straight to the valet. I was leaving too early; all the niggas were pulling up. It looked like a fucking exotic car show. I was texting Liz to tell her not to leave because the boys were coming. When I looked up I noticed a silver GT. Shit, it's Allen, a dude I used to be into, and he looks as sexy as ever. I want to act like I don't see him but it's too late. He shouted out the window and called me over.

I was surprised that he was speaking to me. I wished I could just disappear. I owed him one hundred apologies. I had just walked out on him with no explanation. I knew then I was dead-ass wrong but I really know now. I walked toward his car wondering where the fuck the valet was.

"You're still the baddest thang walking, sexy!" he said, smiling. "So your brother's home now. I know your mom is happy as hell. How you been? I see you ain't changed...you still leave the club early as hell."

"Can you hear me?" He leans closer to the window.

"Yes I can hear you. I'm just trying to figure out where the hell the valet dude is." I paused to gather my thoughts.

"I'm fine Allen, and yes I'm still the baddest thang walking!"

"You are!" he says, getting out of his car.

"How have you and your mom been?"

"I'm good and she's fine, she always asks about you. You should call her sometime. Allen, I'm sorry." I felt so bad that I had never apologized to him. I wanted to explain but this was not the time and I didn't want to sound stupid. I know I needed to say more, but before I could say another word, the valet pulled up.

"Allen, there's my car. I gotta go. Nice seeing you baby."

"Neshela you don't believe in the words I'm sorry, and besides, you don't have to be sorry. I understand you were still in love with him when you took my ring. I always knew you loved him. I wish y'all the best, sexy. Get home safe."

I headed towards the car. If only he knew, I thought. There was no need for the best wishes because Jerri was gone and I was single again. I jumped in my uncle's Maserati and turned up my new favorite song, "Whatever You Like," by T.I. I wanted to block out the thoughts of seeing Allen. I couldn't help thinking what life would have been like if I had stayed with him. I could have learned to love him because I truly enjoyed being around him and he was a good guy. Now I wished I had said more when I had the chance. I should have given him my number, but it was too late. I finally made it my grandmother house; it was already 4:00 a.m. and my flight was scheduled to leave at 9:00. I didn't want to oversleep so I stayed up talking to Hassan while watching reruns on BET.

Chapter 17

All Good Things Come To an End

"I never meant for things to happen this way. I love you Shela"

-Mimi

I was so sick of work, but sponsorship in Atlanta is not easy to find and Hassan is not like Jerri. Working was a must. As I sat at my desk my cell phone began to ring. Mimi and I had been playing phone tag for a week. She called to invite me to a dinner party for her and Quan. It was two days away. Mimi wanted to make an announcement. I suspected that they were getting married, but Mimi didn't give any clues so I didn't pry. I just promised to be there. I immediately started looking for a flight, but a last-minute flight into their small town was over $1,000. Thank God I found a flight to Newark for $585. Rachel or Ivan would have to pick me up. I only had a few days to get myself together and figure out where I was going to send Astar for the weekend. I arranged to send her to Miami while I was in Jersey.

On Friday I rushed to the airport. By the time I got to the gate the plane was leaving. The gate attendant said that another flight was departing at 3:40 from Terminal D, and I was in Terminal A. She printed me a boarding pass and told me to hurry. When I finally got to terminal D that flight had already taken off, and this time no one was there to help me.

I went back to the ticket counter. After 30 minutes of going back and forth with a rude-ass ticket agent, I got a flight that was scheduled to arrive in Newark at 6:55 pm. The flight took forever. It was freezing in Newark. As I exited the plane, I called Rachel to let her know that I had made it. When I made it to the exit Rachel was already standing outside of her truck with open arms.

"So what's the big announcement?"

"I have no idea. Maybe they're expecting."

"I'm thinking they're going to get married."

"I guess we'll see!" said Rachel.

Instead of going directly to Easton, Pennsylvania we went to Rachel's house so that she could finish getting dressed and I could freshen up. Twenty minutes later we were waiting for Low, a good friend of Rachel's. He was riding down to Pennsylvania with us. We finally arrived at The Melt Grill at 10:00. It's a beautiful restaurant that reminded me of Straits, Ludacris's spot in Atlanta. It was decorated in a modern European style and had a warm feel. As the hostess escorted us up the stone staircase to the second floor I noticed the wine racks that covered the walls. About 50 people were in the banquet room. I walked directly to the head of the table to greet Quan and Mimi. I handed them both a greeting card that didn't say anything too specific since I didn't know exactly what we were celebrating. After chatting with Quan and Mimi for a while I sat at the other end of the table.

Mack shouted out, "What up fat girl, you looking kinda good!"

"I always look good baby! I might not be a buck o-five like them little chicks you're used to but I carry this one fifty-six well. Besides, I don't like fat boys!" I tease.

"Whatever Shela, you looking real good tonight!"

"You gonna stop trying me, Mack. Like I said, I always look good!"

"Shit, are those real?" Mack shouts.

Everyone at our end of the table laughed as I placed my hands on my breasts. "Yes, these 36 D's are real! As real as it gets, baby."

The debate ended when the waitress took our orders. As soon as Mack placed his order he was back at it. I was trying to ignore him and made small talk with Rachel and Low. Then Jack, another one of the NJ Boys, started talking to me. He looked a little depressed.

Jack shouted out, "She's right, Mack! She has always been a pretty girl. You're sexy as hell Neshela." He looks me up and down.

"She ain't always been that fine. She's had some work done," Mack shouts.

"Work! You crazy boy, I've always been beautiful!"

"Neshela, you looking real sexy," Jack says.

"Jack, you have always been the sexiest one of the crew, hands down, but you done got too big for me. You look like you're four months pregnant."

"Yeah I have to get it together," he says sadly. "I'm going through a lot right now."

He almost made me feel bad. Oh well, it was too late to take it back. I began talking to Rachel about nothing. Quan and Mimi came to our end of the table. I was thinking they were going to make the big announcement. We still had no clue why we were here. As they walked to the end of the table they stopped and talked to everyone. When they finally reached the very end, Quan said that we need to behave because he could hear our crazy conversation all the way at the other end of the table. I told Quan that Mack had been teasing me. Quan said, "Don't pay these fools no mind Shela. I was getting texts about you and how hot you look tonight. They're just giving you a hard time, sis."

"Whatever Quan, you know Shela had work done!" Mack said, joking.

"Yeah, yeah, Mack and you need a lot of work done," I said. Of course the room went silent. Everyone was eating except me. My food was horrible and there no sense in acting like I liked it. Jack offered me a piece of his steak. I accepted it but it wasn't that good either. Shortly after, the hostess entered the room and asked everyone to meet Quan and Mimi on the third floor. Most of us were surprised because we hadn't noticed that they had left. As the hostess led us to the elevators Jack tried to make small talk with me.

We reached the top floor and the hostess escorted us through the club to a private VIP section. There were bottles of alcohol everywhere and pictures of Quan and Mimi covered the walls. It was obvious that they were announcing their engagement. They stood together and gave a short speech thanking everyone for coming out. Mimi told everyone how Quan had popped the question and showed off her five-carat diamond ring. It was beautiful and she deserved it!

"Y'all have to drink to this," said Quan as he picked up two bottles of Goose. "Shela, you have to drink tonight!" He began pouring Grey Goose as if there was no end. Only a few of us were truly excited about what was going on. Everyone looked shocked or bored to death. It didn't help that the DJ was playing techno.

Even though I vowed to have my second drink on my wedding day, I decided to have it tonight. The room needed some excitement. I shouted to Quan, "Let's drink baby!" Quan was looking shocked. I asked him if he was scared. "We did six shots on my birthday so let's do ten tonight!" Quan threw his hands up. "Whatever girl, you ain't drinking nothing!"

I picked up a glass. Quan poured the first shot. We tossed and I threw back. One down, nine to go. He began pouring drinks for everyone. I called Jack and Mack over to join us. Quan was egging me on, and within a few minutes we had done five shots and emptied the bottle of Goose. Quan signaled for the waitress to bring more bottles. She replaced the Goose with Barley. After shot number 10 I lost count, and Quan poured what was left in the bottle down my throat. He handed me a bottle of water and told me to sit down. The hostess informed us that the club would be closing in 15 minutes. Quan closed the check and we got ready to leave.

Once everyone reached the first floor, it took us a moment to figure out who was riding with whom. I was riding with Quan and Mimi so Rachel wouldn't have to bring me back to her house in Pennsylvania. Rachel and Low were checking on me and calling me crazy. They couldn't believe I drank so much. Low kept asking if I was going to be okay. Rachel insisted that I ride home with them. I told her I was fine, although I could barely stand up.

I was lying across the back seat while Mimi sat in the front. Quan was hanging outside as we waited for Rachel to pull around with my bags. Quan put my bags in the trunk. Jack got in the back seat with me and we went to the freeway.

Jack kept asking me if I was okay. He handed me a bottle of Voss water and told me to drink it. Then he gently started rubbing my hand with the tip of his fingers. It made me a little uncomfortable, so I pulled my hand away as I drank the bottle of water. Then he said that he had to piss. I handed him the Voss water bottle and told him to use it. He complained that the hole was too small. "Yeah, right," I said. "You're from Jersey, plus you're an NJ Boy!" He smiled. Quan pulled onto the shoulder and Jack got out. As the truck came to a stop, I felt nauseous. Reaching for another bottle of water, I hit my head on the seat in front of me. Mimi asked if I was ok. I told Quan and Mimi, "Don't let shit happen to me, y'all." Mimi assured me that nothing was going to happen.

We finally got to Quan and Mimi's house. Quan and Jack got out of the truck leaving Mimi and me. I was not trying to move.

"Chick, you okay?" Mimi asks.

"Mimi I'm fucked up! Don't let shit happen to me."

"Ain't nothing going to happen to you. That's the liquor talking." Mimi giggled.

"Mimi, I'm so happy for y'all! You truly deserve it!"

Quan opened my door. "Y'all come on." He extended his hand to help me out of the truck. Mimi and Quan escorted me through the garage into the kitchen. I was sitting on the bar stool, dazed, as Mimi pulled my boots off. I couldn't stop myself from falling. I was so not feeling this being drunk shit. Everything was moving fast or slow. I lifted myself off the bar stool while holding the counter top to maintain my balance. Mimi shouted, "Don't move, I got you!" and helped me upstairs. Jack stood behind me to make sure I didn't fall. As we reached the top stair I stumbled into the room and onto the bed.

I was out for a few seconds when Jack came to the door to tell me to go to the other room because Shelly, Quan's sister, was going to sleep in the bed that I had just made my home. I couldn't move. "Shela, come on, I got you." Jack helped me off the bed. He pulled me up and guided me to the room across the hall. I kept blacking out for a few seconds at a time, but before I knew it, I was standing in front of the bed. Jack was still holding me close and the room was dark as hell. I could barely see his face but managed to say, "Don't touch me, yo!"

"Shela, I got you, nobody ain't going to mess with you."

"Swear on your life! No, swear on your girl you ain't going to fuck with me."

"I swear! Shela, you okay. Lay down, lay down."

He helped me into the bed in pulled the comforter over me. I melted away into the pillow. This was the oddest feeling I had ever felt in my life. I knew what it was like to be drunk. I could feel my heart beating fast then slow. I felt every vein in my body. I was drifting away and within moments I was sound asleep. Even in my sleep, everything was spinning.

Suddenly someone grabbed my waist. My underwear was being pulled off. Whoever it was started tasting me. The feeling was so good I had to be dreaming. He was blowing in my ass as he held my legs open. It felt so good that it couldn't be right. I was trying to open my eyes but I was too drunk. I just lay there like a corpse as he had his way. I wanted to believe I was dreaming but I knew I wasn't. I was trying to move my body but I couldn't. I felt paralyzed.

As his dick entered me, the thoughts of this feeling good vanished. I was being raped. I was trying to pull away, but my body wouldn't move. I was begging him to stop but no sound came out. My brain was working but my body wasn't responding. Tears ran down my face. At last my eyes opened wide but all I saw was darkness. I tried to shout, "Stop! Please stop, stop!" but it came out softly. As I begged, he placed his hand on my stomach and pushed in hard; it was his last stroke. I thought he was cuming.

I had never felt so dirty. I began to vomit as I pushed myself off the bed and onto the floor. Now I knew what it felt like to be raped. I picked up my cell phone and dialed J's number. No answer. I called Hassan. No answer. I even called Rachel. No one's answering; I just want someone to come and get me. I don't know what to do other than cry myself to sleep.

The early morning sun woke me; I pulled the covers over my head, wishing I could just disappear. I could feel the moisture between my legs. I wish I had kept my ass home. I missed two flights… why didn't I see the signs? I moved around trying to get comfortable on this hard-ass floor, still in disbelief about what had happened to me. I heard Jack's voice asking if I was okay. I saw him sitting in a chair in a corner of the room.

"No, I'm not okay! You took advantage of me!"

"Neshela, I wiped you off, cleaned up your vomit and got you a new cover for your bed," Jack said as if I was saying something crazy.

I held my head confused, knowing inside that what happened was real. My head was killing me. "You RAPED me!" I shouted.

"We are both adults and we were both drunk, and I did stop when you asked me to," Jack said defensively. "I'm sorry, I didn't mean to make you feel no type of way. I never planned to take anything from you."

"Both adults! I was drunk, Jack! I should have never been in your bed! I had no idea that you and I were sleeping in the same bed. In fact, didn't you swear on your girl that you weren't going to bother me when y'all put me in this room? You knew what you were doing. There is no way Quan should have allowed you to rape me in his house. I told Mimi to make sure I was good."

"Rape you? Neshela, I'm sorry you feel that way but you appeared to be enjoying me eating your pussy! And I stopped the moment you asked me to," Jack said. "I have been going through a lot. I haven't been with anyone; sex is the last thing on my mind. I'm sure when Quan put your bags in here last night he didn't think I was going to do anything to you. Y'all family, Neshela. I take full responsibility for what I did and I'm sorry. But don't blame him."

"You knew what you were doing. So I can't understand how you can sit here and be all apologies. So really, I take responsibility for depending on someone else to make sure I was good. Quan and

Mimi aren't family 'cause they would have never put their sisters in a room with you, and they are always talking about how I'm their sister. This shit would have never happened in my house. You have ruined so many relationships! Everybody shows their face. When is the last time you had an AIDS test?!" I walked out of the room and into the bathroom to shower away the sin. My head was still pounding.

As I entered the bathroom I called Rachel. Through tears I told her everything that happened. All she could say was how she wished I had ridden home with her. She didn't know what to do. "Shela I'm so sorry. That's fucked up. I'm calling Mimi right now!" I told Rachel not to say a word. I wanted to wait until I was on my turf, or at least at the airport. I didn't trust any of them anymore.

After spending over an hour in the shower I got dressed and went downstairs. I sat quietly on the couch and everyone was doing their own thing. Not long after it was just Quan and me. "Why did you let him put me in that room?"

Quan barely reacted. "What happens in Cancun stays in Cancun." Before I had a chance to respond, he darted up the stairs. I sat in disbelief. I was mad at myself for not waiting until I was at the airport to bring this up. After all, bitches are showing up dead and no one seems to have a clue why.

At last I told Mimi what had happened at her house. She acted like she had no clue but I knew better. The NJ Boys talk like bitches; I was sure it was pillow talk last night. I was yelling and crying at the same time. I had never been so hurt. I finally give her a chance to respond. She said she was sorry and then she went on to say that she had been with me all the way. She says she put me on the bed and made sure all of my bags were in the room with me in case I needed anything.

"Shelly was supposed to sleep on the couch. You were never supposed to sleep in Jack's room." She continued, "When I saw Jack pacing the floor I didn't think anything but when I watched him pull you across the hall, I felt that something was wrong. I told Quan and he told me to mind my business. Shela, I'm sorry! I had no idea." We were both crying. "Neshela, I'm sorry. I'm gonna get to the bottom of this. Let me call Quan and I'm gonna call you right back." Mimi had just said a mouthful. Quan told her to mind her own business. Now I was pissed and wishing I had dialed 911. Quan knew exactly what went on.

Mimi called back. I didn't bother to answer her call because I didn't want to talk about it. I'd already told her how I felt. Mimi and Quan kept calling. I had nothing to say to them. Shortly after their calls I received a few text messages from Quan saying he had no idea and asking if we could talk. Mimi had told him that something was wrong. Jack said that Quan put my bags in his room and told him that I was going to sleep there the whole time. Who knew if Jack was telling the truth, but I was sure that Mimi was. She said it! She said: Quan told her to mind her business.

Moments later I received a voicemail from Mimi. "Neshela we've been trying to call you. Please call me back. Shela, I love you like a sister. We have been through so much together. I am truly sorry, please call me. Your brother and I want to talk to you. I'm sorry, Shela. It should have never happened! I'm sorry, we're sorry! Let's fix this, please. We're family. I love you."

It's nice to know that she was sorry now, but she watched him pull me across the hall into his room. They turned away while I was raped in their house. Now they wanted to talk about it. Fucking amazing. **I hoped they all burned in hell!**

Chapter 18

Problems

"Some bridges are meant to be burnt because there's no need to cross them ever again in life"

-Neshela

I'll never forget October 9th. I hadn't been the same since the rape. I was still waiting for my test results to come back, praying that I didn't I have any STDs. Only God knows what that nasty bastard had. All of me wondered when Mimi and Quan lost respect for me. I would have never guessed in a million years that this shit would have happened to me in their house. I kept hearing Quan say, "What happens in Cancun, stays in Cancun," and Mimi saying, "Quan told me to mind my business." I couldn't help thinking that it was all planned, but why?

My cell phone interrupted my thoughts. It seemed too early for someone to be calling me, but it was Hassan calling me back from the other night. I hadn't been talking to anyone, and when I needed him the most, he hadn't answered. When I pressed the talk button he started checking on me. I wanted to tell him what happened, but I was too embarrassed. He said he really needed to talk to me, so he was boarding a flight in two hours. I didn't understand his urgency, but regardless I couldn't wait to see him. I wondered if he knew. But I had so much on my mind. I couldn't help thinking of Jerri. No matter how many years pass, October was always a rough month for me. Now I have another painful memory to add to dark October: the memory of being raped.

I was just leaving the doctor's office. My results had come back, and thank God I didn't have anything. Afterwards I had to pick up Hassan at the airport. It was a rainy day. I got to the airport and Hassan was walking out of the door. We went to the W hotel in Dunwoody. When we entered the room he began to kiss me all over while pulling my clothes off. He laid me gently on the bed and made love to me. I was so disconnected; it didn't feel right. I didn't want him to think something was wrong, so I lay in position and allowed him to enjoy the moment. He was only staying for a day which was great because my mother was flying up to spend a few weeks with Astar and me.

While we lay in bed talking about the future, Hassan told me of his plan to retire. I had never asked him about his work. I guess I already knew that he was a hustler, but eventually I knew he would realize that there was no future in that line of business. I was just thinking about how much I enjoyed being beside him. Hassan woke me early the next morning. He said he was going to take a cab to the airport. Before he left he made love to me one more time. When I finally woke up it was 10:00 a.m., and I had to rush home to get things ready for my mother.

My mother's flight landed at 7:30 and Astar was so excited to see her grandmother. We sat in the car quietly as we drove to my house. My mother and I had come so far; at one point in my life I barely spoke to her. But as an adult I respected her and the decision she made. Now my mother and I talk all the time. I have learned that she is the one person that will always be honest with me.

The first few days were great, but a week and a half in I was so ready for her to go home. I hate house guests—I don't know what I was thinking when I agreed to have her for three weeks. For some odd reason I thought I would enjoy my mother's company and I did, for the first four days at least. Now it was time to go. Astar was acting like a spoiled brat and the temperature in my house changed from 30 below to 90 degrees all in one hour. I was dying and I felt like I was catching the flu. I wanted to tell my mother to go home. Astar was acting like a different kid. I wanted to beat her ass so bad.

Thank God Hassan was coming on Friday. I couldn't wait to get out of this house. I felt like a prisoner. The days were not going by fast enough between my job, my mom and Astar. Everything was bothering me.

I was bundled up on the couch as if it was 30 below. The little red dial on my thermostat was as low as it could go. I was trying to watch "House," one of my favorite shows. When I heard a loud bang at the door, I was wishing it was God answering my prayer with a pilot to take my mother home. "Who is it?" I shouted.

"U.S. Marshals, open the door!" I felt a chill run down my spine as I opened the door. "Are you Neshela Jones?"

"Yes." At this point my mother was next to me.

"You're under arrest for the murder of Jerri Hopkins." The officer read me my rights and cuffed me. I asked if I could at least put on a pair of shoes. My mother started saying the Lord's Prayer and the 23rd Psalm. I couldn't believe this was happening. As the Marshal began pulling me out of the doorway, two other officers entered my house. My mother looked them both in the eyes.

"You have a warrant to arrest my baby, so then take her. But you will not come in this house without a warrant. So with all due respect, get out!" Then she shouted to me, "Neshela, don't say a word, I will call the lawyer! Keep saying the Lord's Prayer, Psalms 23 and 91. God is the only one that can help you. Keep your mouth closed. It will be okay! Don't say a word!"

I was under arrest for the murder of a man that I loved. The officer placed me in that back seat of unmarked police car. We took a long trip to Fulton county jail. After I was fingerprinted, the corrections officer directed me to a blue wall. She told me to bend over, hold my ass cheeks open, and cough twice. Then she had me turn around and open my mouth so that she could examine me as if I was at the doctor's office. Moments later she placed me into a holding cell where I waited to be extradited to the Essex County Jail. The transfer took a few days; I flew to New Jersey on a Continental flight with two corrections officers. From the airport it was a fifteen-minute drive to the hell hole. It took over four hours for them to book me again. This time I got a green jumpsuit and a cell.

Jeff, my lawyer, finally visited me and we went over the case. He was still waiting for the discovery from the DA's office. We went over my alibi again and again; I had been at home with Astar in the early morning hours of October 30. I told Jeff, "They can pull my phone records. I called Jerri from my house phone at 3:00 a.m. There is no way I could have been in Jersey at the same time. Besides, what was my motive? I loved him with all my heart. I really don't know what happened to him."

Jeff asked questions about Jerri 's lines of business, the insurance policy, money flowing through my accounts. Then the big question.

Jeff said, "Neshela, I need you to be honest. I'm your lawyer and I will be representing you. These are serious charges. You've been charged with first degree murder. From the little we know, it looks like the case is based on information from an informant.

They were painting it as a drug deal gone wrong. Neshela, did you have anything to do with Jerri 's business affairs?"

"I didn't know anything about what Jerri did. We talked about lots of things, but his business was none of mine. I would never allow anyone to incriminate me. I might help him count money every now and then, but that's it. Of course I know what went out in the black bag or shoes boxes. But we never talked about those things. We had so many other things to talk about, Jeff. Our relationship wasn't like that at all; I don't know where people came up with those stories. I wasn't his connect. I *wasn't*."

My visit with Jeff ended and I was sent back to my cell. I could never understand where the DA came up with these stories. The new story was that I was Jerri's fucking connect; I was supposed to be the middle man. First it was my family, now it's a nigga I was fucking. Wow, these people are crazy! I was sitting on my cot when my cellmate Gina started talking to me.

Gina was a Puerto Rican chick from the Bronx. She was encouraging as hell and at this point I needed it. Like me, Gina had a murder charge; unlike me, she did it. She killed her stepfather who had molested her for most of her life. Gina said that she just woke up one morning and shot her father in the head five times. Then she cut his dick off and put it in his mouth. She called the police on herself. It sounded crazy, but I guess that's what she needed to do. She was just twenty years old. She pleaded not guilty, but at the end she confessed. She was waiting to be transferred to Clinton Prison. She got 30 years.

Gina told so many stories about her childhood. Her father was a pimp and her mother was his bottom bitch. Her mother died of AIDS when Gina was ten, and by the time Gina turned thirteen, her step father was pimping her and fucking her. With her mother gone, there was no one to protect her. She took her mother's spot in no time; Gina said that she was the bottom bitch at fourteen. All the other hoes hated her. Gina was 5'7" with long, wavy brown hair and the body of a stripper. Her body was that of a grown woman but when she opened her mouth, she was a little girl. Sometimes I would just listen to her go on and on. Gina's stories would put me to sleep.

Chapter 19

Caught Up

"Being caught up with no escape is the worst feeling"

-Rob

I didn't have a bond, so the Essex County jail, known to everyone around as the Green Monster, was my new home. I was arraigned, but no trial date had been set. Everyone seemed to be supportive, but my brother told me that it would wear off sooner or later. He told me to be strong, but I didn't know how much longer I could do this. I wanted to go home; I needed to see my daughter. I asked my mother not to bring her to the jail though. When my brother went to jail we told the kids that he was going off to college. I wouldn't know where to begin explaining jail to Astar.

Rachel came to visit me; it was nice seeing her. I didn't have any friends in New Jersey. My cousin Nish came to visit me; she lived in upstate New York and was the closest family I had. When I lived in Newark with Jerri I would talk to her all the time. Nish is more like a big sister. She tried to talk me out of that abortion. When I told her about being pregnant with Moon she was the only person who laid it on me. She told me how selfish I was and how I only enjoyed the benefits of my relationship. She was right—at the time I loved Jerri, but I was not willing to have his baby or wait for him if he went to prison. Nish's husband had got a bid, and, like any down-ass chick, she held him down. That shit didn't make any sense to me, but now that I was in jail, I had a new understanding.

Jeff usually called on Thursdays with updates about the case. Nothing much had changed. Today I was hoping Jeff had some different news for me. He told me that he thought it was bigger than we knew. However, he was pushing for a dismissal because the DA's case was shaky and he couldn't believe that a judge gave the DA a warrant based on circumstantial evidence. He made it clear that the DA's case seemed odd, but he thought that there was an indictment prior to Jerri's murder. Jeff thinks the state was buying time and holding me in jail so the Feds could come and question me. None of it made any sense to me. I was not worried about the Feds because I knew that I had nothing to do with any drugs or any drugs deals.

When I returned to my cell I was confident. I had so much to look forward to. Jeff was shooting for the dismissal. I sat on the cot, praying and thanking God that I would be going home. Gina started telling a story. She was talking my ear off when the corrections officer called me for visitation; I was surprised because I wasn't expecting anyone. When I finally got downstairs I saw Hassan. How did he know that I was here? I picked up the phone. He placed his hand on the glass. "I miss you." I was excited to see him but not like this. I looked a mess and I had lost weight. It took me a second to gather my thoughts. "How did you know I was here?"

"Everyone knows you're here. The streets talk." Then he asked if I had seen Mimi and Quan.

He didn't know that I wasn't speaking to them anymore. I ignored his question. "So what are the streets saying?"

"You already know, some people think you know what happened. Other people think it's fucked up that you're in the middle of this. You know the street, people just talking."

"So what do you think? Do you think I had something to do with this?"

"Why you asking me that? You think I'd be here if I thought you killed my man? Really Shela, you think I would lie next to you if I didn't trust you? I know why he loved you. The same reason why I..." The corrections officer came over the loudspeaker and cut Hassan off. "Wrap it up. Visits are over in fifteen minutes."

"What does your lawyer think? Hassan asked.

"He doesn't know. He said the case is bigger than we know. He thinks there was an indictment that came out before Jerri got killed. Maybe that was the motive for the murder or the suicide." I didn't want to tell him too much.

"It'll be okay. I got my people to bring you some real food today. If you need anything, let me know. You know where to call me. I already set up an account with the corrections billing service, so call as much as you want. I got to go, but I'll see you in a few days." He blew me a kiss as he walked away.

Back in the cell, Gina was sitting on her bed wanting to know who the visitor was. I told her all about Green Eyes. Then she handed me a red rose she said that a trustee dropped by for me. I smiled knowing that it came from Hassan. Within thirty minutes a corrections officer called me to a back room where he handed me a McDonald's bag. The old me would have handed the bag back. I was not a fan of fast food, but the new Neshela said thank you. I was so grateful; I had never eaten a burger and fries so fast in my life. I brought a small piece back for Gina. We began to have fast food a few times a week. Hassan had a cell phone smuggled in to me so now I could make all the calls I wanted. I didn't have to wait in line for the phone anymore.

Jeff couldn't get a date on the court calendar to argue my dismissal, so I was still praying and hoping for the best. I don't know what I would have done without Hassan. He visited me twice a week to keep my spirits up and every few days he had one of the officers bring me some real food. I had been taking those diet pills that Quan had given me up until the day the Marshal picked me up. But the jailhouse diet was the best; I lost at least fifteen pounds. But now I was gaining it back with all the Mickey D's and BK burgers.

Chapter 20

Jail Letters to Jerri

"Fuck love, I can't wait to get the hell out of this place"

-Neshela

I thought I was dying. Even with all of the new luxury that I had, I was becoming depressed. I hated this place. I was at the lowest point in my life; I didn't want to live anymore. I started throwing up. Every morning I woke up with my head in the toilet. Gina said I should see the nurse, but I didn't want to. I was just homesick. I was sick of this place and I was sick of Gina and her stories. Lately she kept arguing with the corrections officer about not being transferred. She said she should have been transferred by now and that it usually only took two weeks after sentencing. I had been here for three weeks and Gina was sentenced the day before I came. I really didn't want her to leave yet. Gina's crazy ass kept me sane, but I was sick of hearing her complain.

They say you get what you ask for. I fell asleep listening to Gina tell another one of her crazy stories. When I woke up this morning she was gone. I thought I was dreaming last night when I saw Gina walking out of the cell; I guess I was knocked out. She was transferred last night to the women's prison. I didn't even hear her leave; now I had the cell to myself. All I could think about was 30 years in prison. If they gave me 30 years I would just kill myself. I could get life in prison for a crime that I didn't commit. Thirty years is life to me. Wishing I was dead already, I called Melissa. I was contemplating suicide because life could not get any worse. Melissa and I talked for about an hour and then my cell phone died. The officer that recharged my phone was off so I was stuck. Shit! It was good that I talked to Melissa because she had a lot of positive things to say. I needed to hear them.

November 15, 2008

It's been so long since we've talked. I miss you so much. Jerri, I wish you were here. I need you J, I need you so bad right now. Baby I can't do this alone. This shit is crazy. I can't see Astar, I don't have any picture of us to look at, and I want to die. If it wasn't for Astar I would just hang myself baby. If you did it baby, I swear I understand how it feels. I can truly say that I know how it feels not to want to live. Jerri, I understand.

November 16, 2008

I'm lying here, thinking of you, and at this moment I wish I never met you because I wouldn't be here. Jerri, I'm in jail accused of your murder and I don't understand why. This is not fair J, and you know it. They pulled me out of my house they arrested me and charged me with your murder. If your tired-ass baby mom got anything to do with this I swear Jerri, I'm going to bury that bitch alive.

November 20, 2008

I'm still here but I guess you already know that. Jerri I hate this place, I just want to go home baby. What have I ever done to deserve this? Why are they doing this to me?

Chapter 21

The Truth

"And ye shall know the truth, and the truth shall make you free."

-John 8:32 KJV

I was sitting on the cot, thinking of my daughter. Out of the blue, a corrections officer called me out of my cell for a visitor. It was Monday and my visits were on Wednesday, Saturday and Sunday. I was thinking it was the Feds, but they would just transfer me to their facility. When I got to the private visiting areas, the corrections officer uncuffed me and pushed me into the room. I glared back at him, not noticing the man in the corner.

"Hey lady, how are you holding up?' It was Albie.

"Albie! I'm good, considering. No, I wish I would fucking die. I hate this place!"

"You'll be okay. I know a few officers here and told them you're my family."

"Thanks Albie."

"Well Neshela, I'm going to be honest with you. I heard some talk around the office. I had no idea you've been here for so long. The case is a joke; they can't prove anything against you. I wouldn't be telling you this if I didn't know you were innocent. You need to give me your word that you won't tell anyone what I'm about to tell you. It is straight from the case file, the file that no one can see, not even your lawyer." Albie had me scared as hell at this point. What could it be?

"You must take this information to your grave. If it gets too sticky I will do what I can, but don't expect much." Albie went on for an hour about Jerri and the case, but the last ten minutes was the most essential part. He said Shitara was the major player in the case against me. She was the informant and so was her fiancé,

Hassan Mahatma, aka Green Eyes. I was stunned. It was obvious that Albie didn't know of my relationship with Hassan. He was trying to describe him from his mug shot. Albie's description was a little off, but I knew exactly who he was talking about. Albie explained that Jerri's suicide had been ruled a murder, so $825,000 of insurance was to be paid. Little did I know when Shitara talked to me earlier this year she just wanted to know what I knew.

Albie said she told the detective that she didn't think that Jerri had made me the beneficiary of his insurance policy, that I told her that I was Jerri 's connect and I had no control over his death, and that the murder was a hit by my boss. She told the officer that the killing was supposed to look like murder, but the other hit man got out of the car too early so she thinks Jerri had to kill himself, knowing that if he didn't kill himself, his family would die in his place. She told the detective that I told her all of these things. She even had the phone records to prove that she had talked to me for over seven hours. Albie also said that Shitara told the detective that she was Jerri's wife and they were planning their wedding and planning to have more children. She said that she moved back in with her mother because she and Jerri were looking for a new place in Pennsylvania. Of course the detective looked into everything, and indeed there were four insurance policies in Jerri 's name. One policy was worth $500,000, two were worth $150,000 and one was $25,000. However, they never found a marriage certificate for Jerri and Shitara.

The only one I knew of was the $500,000 one. We got the policies together. I tried to tell Albie that Jerri and I got separate insurance policies, each worth $500,000, when I was pregnant with the twins. He asked if I was sure that I was the beneficiary to Jerri's insurance. I had no clue. "To my knowledge I am, but I didn't stand over his shoulder as he filled out the paperwork, so I have no idea. I just know that everything you just told me is a lie."

"Neshela, tell your lawyer as much as you can without making it obvious that someone told you. I wish you the best, but I have to get out of here." Then he asked, "Neshela, the detective was looking for you for five months. She gave them your home address. How did she get it?"

"I don't know. Thank you for everything."

"No problem, baby girl! If you get a new cellmate, don't talk to her!"

I placed my hands on my head. All I could think about was Hassan. He played me, sitting across the table from me every week, making sure I was good, acting all concerned. This fucking nigga! I looked up to heaven and called out to Jerri, "Baby please help me." The officer came into the room. "Sorry to interrupt your prayer, but let's go!" She cuffed me and we went back to the unit. I entered my cell with no one to talk to. I wish Gina were here. My cell phone was dead so I couldn't call anyone. I picked up my pad and wrote to Jerri.

> Jerri,
>
> First and foremost, I'm sorry. I don't what I was thinking, Jerri. He showed up at a time when I was needy. He played the good guy role and I fell for it. Jerri, I had no

intentions of falling for him. I was just...no, he was just befriending me at first. At least that's what I thought. Jerri, I'm sorry baby! It all just happened so fast.

My cries fell on deaf ears; I couldn't feel Jerri. In fact, I hadn't felt him or seen a sign from him in months. I felt hopeless and I couldn't even tell anyone about the whole situation because then I would have to tell everyone about Hassan. He fucking played me! I felt so used that I just didn't want to deal with the reality. Fuck, even Kevin smelled this shit from far away, and he didn't even really know Hassan! If it wasn't for the officers waking me to make sure I was alive at shift change I would just sleep the days away. I couldn't wait to get out of this place.

The trustee came by to drop off my rose as she did every few days, but today she handed me a white rose and apologized for it not being red. I just looked at it and went back to sleep. I didn't want anything from Hassan. In fact, I lost track of the days until an officer called me for a visit.

Everything made so much sense to me now. I sat in my cell for two days and analyzed my relationship with Hassan. I thought of the day that Hassan made it to the hotel before me. The airport was at least 40 minutes from Dunwoody and I only lived 15 minutes away, but Hassan was at the hotel when I got there. Obviously, he was already in Atlanta. Also, how did Shitara get my home address? He had to have seen my address on my mail that day that I left it in the seat of my car.

I'd been in jail for forty five days. Jeff hadn't gotten me out and I was sick as a dog. I was back to throwing up every morning. I thought I had a stomach virus, and in addition to throwing up I had the runs too. I felt horrible and I looked it. This place was killing me. I tried to pull myself together. The officers called me for a visit again and I was sure it was Hassan.

I was right, but he wasn't all smiles. I asked what was wrong. "I can't tell you on this phone." I wanted to care that something was wrong with him, but I couldn't allow myself to.

"So if things are so bad, why are you here?"

"Because I don't miss a visit with you, my lady! What's wrong with you?"

"Nothing. My stomach just hurts."

I continued to make small talk. I was sure he could tell I was distracted. This role was difficult for me. I told Hassan that I was not feeling well so I cut our visit short. When I returned to my cell I had mail from my brother and a card from Christopher. I sat on my cot and started reading through them, hoping that they would cheer me up. I opened the one from Christopher first.

Hey Neshela, I hope this card find you well. I wish you all the best, and stay strong!

—Love Christopher

P.S., Holla if you need me baby.

It was nice to see that even though Chris and I had ended things a long time ago, he hadn't forgotten about me. I also wanted to see what Rob wrote to me. He had been in my position before.

Ay baby it's going to be okay. You got to be strong. I never imagined you on this side of the bars but don't worry, we will get you out of there. Pray, sleep, read the Bible, and the days will go by faster, I promise. Stay strong, White Girl.

-Rob

I took my brother's advice and slept the days away. I lost track of the days until the officer called me for a visit. It was so hard for me to keep acting, but he was playing his role and I respected the grimy-ass nigga for that. I truly respect people that are the best at what they do. He'd thought this one out; he got me—he and that bitch, Shitara!

When I got to the visitation room I was expecting to see Hassan, but it was Ghost. I was so depressed and I knew he could see it. There was no sense in asking Ghost how he knew I was in jail. He always knew everything. After about three minutes, Ghost said, "Melissa told me you were here. She told me that you were talking about killing yourself and she hadn't heard from you in a few days. She's worried about you, Neshela. What's going on?'

"Nothing." I said it so quietly that I don't know if he even heard me.

"I had my lawyer look into your case. He said that the case is all hearsay and he doesn't understand why your lawyer hasn't filed for a dismissal."

"I don't know why, Ghost. How did Melissa know?" She didn't know about my relationship with Ghost. I was dying to know how Melissa knew and what made her call him.

"I didn't ask, I was just surprised when she called. I didn't even know you knew her. She begged me not to tell you that she told. I told her I wouldn't, so don't say a word to her." I gave him my word that I wouldn't say anything to Melissa.

"She's just looking out for you. I want you to fire your lawyer so I can put Richard on your case. He said he'll have you out of here by next week. You look a mess! Pull yourself together, yo! I know its murder, but you know you didn't do it. So look on the bright side—you can cash in that insurance policy! I'll make a few investments for you." He placed two fingers on his lips, kissed them, then placed his fingers on my forehead. Ghost was my nigga no matter what.

"I need you to be your old sassy self. Don't worry about anything. I'm going to get you out of here. I was going to treat you like one of my clients. Melissa will be your point of contact. My wife would die if she knew, so we have to keep this on the low. I'll keep Melissa posted on everything." Considering Melissa is already aware of our relationship, I didn't see this to be a problem. Ghost was a high-profile sports agent; he signed all the top players. Melissa as the middle man was a great idea; he didn't need me calling him from jail.

"That's fine, but I'm broke. I spent my last $20,000 on Jeff's fees. I can't afford Richard."

"I said I got this. I got to get you out of here." When I got back to my cell there was a red rose on my cot. I flushed it down the toilet. I hated Hassan. My talk with Ghost was exactly what I needed, a reminder of who I was: Neshela Jones.

I thought about home. It took a lot for me not to see my baby girl, but I couldn't let her see me like this. I missed her more each day. I missed everybody. I couldn't wait to go home, but I needed to stay focused.

Chapter 22

Final Days

"I'll always take care of you I love you, Neshela Jones"

-Ghost

Just as Ghost promised, Richard was on my case, and within three days Richard had me in court with a motion for a dismissal. The judge granted the motion; due to lack of evidence, the case against me was dismissed. My friends and family were rejoicing, but some people shook their heads in disbelief. It took me a second to understand what was going on. I sighed with relief. I was a free woman and thanking God. I had so much to be grateful for. I stood motionless giving thanks to The Creator.

As the tears rolled from my eyes, I couldn't help but think of Jerri; through all of the pain, I still missed him. It took a few hours before I was released, but I finally walked out of the Green Monster. To my surprise, it was Quan who came to pick me up. I paused, trying to figure out whose bright idea this was. I guess no one knew what had happened a month before. The moment I got in the car, Quan said, "Shela I'm sorry, that shit should have never happened. I should have made sure you were good. I should have stayed on top of things." I just asked him to take me to Fairmount Cemetery. I wanted to say goodbye to Jerri. I had no plans of returning to Newark. Quan stopped at the florist across from the cemetery so that I could get roses. I laid four dozen white and red roses for the man I loved.

This visit was shorter than usual. Maybe it was because Quan was waiting for me. I will always love Jerri, but I could not go back to this place. Newark filled my soul with pain and carried memories I couldn't bear. I decided it would be the end of the graveyard visits for me; I had to close this chapter in my life. With all of the unanswered questions and not knowing who to trust, I was done with dirty Jersey. I had to let go. I knew in reality that Jerri was not there. His spirit was among the people that he loved, so I had no reason to come back here. As I climbed back into the truck, I wiped my tears, knowing that I was finally over it.

Quan and I went to Rachel's house to pick up Rachel and Mimi. Quan, Mimi and Rachel were taking me to dinner at Mr. Chow's. It took us over an hour to get to Manhattan. I couldn't wait to eat some real food. We were an hour late for our reservation. There had been a few modifications since the last time I was here with Jerri, but Mr. Chow's always reminded me of a scene out of *Scarface.* It was just something about the dramatic dining room and black varnish. It was the only restaurant I had ever been to that didn't have menus. I loved this place!

I remembered when Jerri and I would drive to Manhattan just to have dinner here. I'll never forget the day when we came here with Melissa and Malik. Jerri and Melissa wanted to pay our $1,158 check in singles. I was so embarrassed and Jerri knew it. After giving the server a bundle of dollar bills he called him back and exchanged the singles with hundreds.

As we waited for the host to greet us I stared off in space, reminiscing about the time I spent with Jerri at this very place. Rachel nudged me and asked if I was ok. She directed my attention to one of the servers that walked passed us. She wanted me to get a look at him. "He's so handsome," she said. We giggled as we continued walking towards the table. I didn't even notice that everyone was here: Liz, Melissa and my cousin Nish from New York. I was so happy to see all of my friends and family. I was even more surprised to see Wesley at the other end of the table, considering he had found out that I knew all the lies he'd told about me.

We spent over three hours at Mr. Chow's that evening chatting and enjoying dinner. We ordered an assortment of Beijing dishes and the night was going well until I suddenly found myself in the bathroom stall with my head in the bowl. Vomit was everywhere. I wasn't sure if it was the duck or the fresh sea bass. I just knew my stomach was killing me.

After dinner, I just wanted to find a bed to lie in, but I had to fly back to Atlanta where my daughter and mother were waiting. I planned to sleep right by Astar's side tonight. When I went to jail, my mother stepped right in just as she did for my brother. She moved into my house so that Astar wouldn't have to miss school or deal with another change. I didn't know how I would ever be able to repay her.

It had been a little over a week since I was released from jail. I still wasn't feeling well so I decided to make a doctor's appointment. I had probably caught a disease from that nasty-ass cell. When I told the doctor that I thought I had a stomach virus, he returned with a smile on his face and the news that I was 11 weeks pregnant. I couldn't believe it. My stomach virus turned out to be morning sickness. Still in disbelief, I walked out of the doctor's office with two prescriptions and a congratulations package.

Chapter 23

Sunshine Through Darkness

"You can always see the sun shining through the darkness"
-Neshela

I hadn't talked to Hassan since my release, but being pregnant changed everything. I waited a few days before I called to share the news with him. When I finally told him, he insisted that I fly to Jersey right away. I declined; I told him I needed to be with Astar. Besides, she was spending her entire winter break with her pappy in Miami. I had to put him off for a few weeks because I wasn't ready to deal with the whole thing. I thought that would be a better time for us to see each other and it was only a few weeks away.

I still couldn't believe I didn't even realize I was pregnant. The more I thought about it, this pregnancy reminded me of the time when I was pregnant with Moon. I had the worst morning sickness, my stomach would constantly churn, and I was always nauseous. While I was in jail Gina told me I should see the nurse but I really thought it was just homesickness. I never imagined it could be this, a baby!

As I sat on the bed, I analyzed the whole situation. Then I got a call from Rob. I hadn't talked to him in a few days, but ever since I escaped the Green Monster, it seemed like we had been talking almost every day. I told him about the baby, and he was adamant that I move back to Miami. I was considering it after I got released, but now that I'm pregnant I just had to figure out what was the best solution for the baby. I promised to God and Jerri that I would never have another abortion.

Lying down on my bed, I began to think about everything I've been through this past year. Though it all pained me, the worst part was that Jerri's murder was still unsolved. I don't think I'll ever be able to have a good night's sleep until I know for sure what happened. And now this situation with Hassan has become even more complicated. I wondered, did I bring this upon myself? I should have never slept with him. I wished I had listened to Kevin; he told me to be careful. I fell for that lying motherfucker! And now I have no clue what I'm going to do. I'm just happy to be free.

Chapter 24

Getting Things Lined Up

"Without order, is chaos"

-Neshela

It was Christmas Eve and Astar was leaving for Miami to spend the holidays with her pappy. I hated to let her go, but he only gets to see her on holidays and during the summer. We arrived at the airport early to give us extra time to get past the holiday rush. It took more than an hour to get through the TSA security line. Within a few minutes the flight attendant began to board the flight. Astar was first to board because she was an unaccompanied minor. I sat at the gate watching Astar's flight become airborne. I usually watch Astar's plane until I can't see it and then head home, but today Hassan was flying into town. I was just going to wait around at the airport and surprise him at the gate. I had a little more than an hour to waste.

I was three months pregnant by a man that set me up. Even if I wanted to believe that he cared for us, I couldn't. I still had to play my role. When Hassan's flight landed I didn't see him. I called him. "Baby I'm getting off the plane right now. I'll be out front in a few minutes." I was looking right at him. He started to smile when he saw me. I smiled back, holding all the hurt inside. I hated him.

The first few days were normal; Hassan was staying for two weeks. This was the longest period of time he had ever stayed at my place. He'd only been here a few times because I hated bringing him here to Jerri 's spot. Hassan had no place here, but I had to stay focused. After all, he was the father of my unborn child.

As I prepared dinner, Hassan walked into the kitchen to help. He peeled potatoes while I placed meatloaf into the oven. It killed me inside that he was so nice and helpful. He played this role better than I could ever imagine. After the potatoes boiled we mashed them. I set the table and we ate dinner. It was Christmas Eve, and to my surprise, Hassan pulled a gift from under the table. I was shocked. He had made it very clear that he didn't celebrate holidays. It was a small blue box from Tiffany's. I opened it right away. It was a beautiful Legacy Collection ring with an aquamarine stone and a diamond-encrusted platinum band, the exact ring I had been wanting for so long. Attached was a small note that read, "Thanks for helping me love again." What a fucking liar.

I looked at him and said thanks. I placed the ring on my right index finger. He chuckled and kept eating. After dinner Hassan watched me clean the kitchen and after I finished we walked into my bedroom and went to sleep. As much as I hated him, I loved being in his arms. When I woke up on Christmas morning, Hassan was still sound asleep. I began to slide out of bed, but he pulled me close. Moments later I escaped. I washed my face and brushed my teeth. Even though Hassan didn't celebrate Christmas I planned to serve breakfast in bed in a cute Santa outfit.

I put the meal together fast and pulled his gift from the front closet. I ran into Astar's room to change into my costume. I walked back into the kitchen to place his food on the tray. I placed the tray on my side of the bed, and then I crawled close to him so that I could feed him. When he turned and noticed me he smiled and pulled me close while placing me on his lap. He began to kiss my neck slowly and one thing led to another. After the greatest sex ever, I handed Hassan his gift: a Breitling Bentley

6.75—a grown man watch. He kissed my forehead and made love to me one more time.

We spent the next few days doing nothing. Today was the first day that we had been out of the house. We had an appointment with my OB/GYN. We were going to get a 3-D ultrasound and see our new baby. Hassan wanted a girl; I didn't care, as long as the baby was healthy. After the doctor's visit we headed to Seasons 52 and then we picked out a few movies from Blockbuster and drove back to the house. I only had a few more days to enjoy being by his side, so I was cherishing every moment, mostly for our child. I can live without him, but I felt so sorry for my baby. This was the abortion that I was supposed to have but couldn't.

It was Wednesday, December 31, 2008. Most people were excited about the New Year's but Hassan was a Muslim so we didn't celebrate. Being with Hassan was not at all like being with Jerri. With J, we would celebrate just because. But I was going to celebrate anyway. I was just waiting on the roofie that I placed in his drink to settle in his body and then I would rejoice. I had waited so long for this day.

When I noticed his delayed reactions, I jumped on his lap and began to kiss him, acting all concerned. I kept asking him what was wrong. I touched his forehead as if I was checking to see if he had a fever. In a few seconds he was out. I took his gun from his side of the bed and placed it in the dishwasher. Then I opened the door for Rob who had brought all the material I needed. We tied Hassan to the bed. I told Rob that I wanted to do this on my own. As I walked him out he handed me a CK 45 with a silencer. I thanked my brother as I closed and locked the door. He said, "You got to do this, I'll be nearby. Call me when you're done."

"I will Rob, I got this!" I closed the door and walked swiftly back to my room. Hassan was still out. I wanted him to wake up. I took the butt of the gun and struck him across the head. "Wake the fuck up! Fuck, nigga!" His eyes opened wide, but it took him a second to realize what was going on.

"Baby what are you doing?"

"Bitch ass nigga, don't 'baby' me! You know what time it is! "

"What are you doing?"

I hit him with the butt of the gun again. "You tell me what's going on. I know everything, but I want to hear it from you. I want to hear it from *you*." I was stuttering. The pain of killing the man I love was killing me. I was no killer but I stared hard at him so he would think that I was.

"I'm sorry! I didn't kill him. He did it himself; I guess that's what he wanted! I couldn't put a bullet in my man's head. He was alive the last time I seen him. I met up with him that day to get some shit. I didn't even know nothing was wrong, and when I got out of the car he seemed fine. He was alive, I swear on Allah! Please believe me. Just untie me I'll tell you the whole story. I'll tell you whatever you want to know."

He had been in the car? If I untied him he'd tell me everything? Did he really know what happened to J.? Everything had changed.

Maybe he had killed J. What had I gotten myself into? I hit him a third time, for J.

"What do you mean when you got out of the car? What time did you meet him? Who was there? You left him there to get killed?" I didn't want to hear anymore. I wanted Hassan dead. My God, these secrets were killing me.

Shitara had told the police that it was a hit and one person had gotten out of the car early. Maybe she had been telling me the truth, considering she and Hassan set me up. I was sure she didn't have anything to do with Jerri's death. I was confused about everything. Nothing was making sense. I was looking at him with rage.

"I love you, don't do this to us!" he pleaded. "I wanted to tell you but I couldn't. You know the code of the streets. Don't do this to us. I really love you and I want us to work, that's why I'm here."

"Want us to work!" I whacked him across the head with the butt of the gun with all of my strength. Blood poured from the gash on his forehead. "You tried to play me! Hassan, remember you'll never love again. Why did you kill him? Why? You killed so many people that day. Why?" I shout. "Answer me!"

He pleaded, "I told you, I didn't kill him, I met up with J on Broad Street to get a package early that day. When I left he was alive. Emmet was in the car with him. I was only there for a minute because I had shit to take care of. Neshela it wasn't me, I didn't kill him. He killed himself. Shela, money wasn't the same and

Jerri's open case would only make things bad for everyone. Everyone knew the Feds were watching him. "

"What are you talking about? What open case?"

"Shela, J was going to court with Allen. They were co-defendants but Allen decided to cooperate with the Feds and testify against J. Allen knew everything about J's operation and he told it all, even taping conversations between him and Jerri. Long story short, J was looking at 30 years if he didn't snitch on the connect and, from my understanding, that was supposed to be you. But you know that I know better. Shit, he was going broke on top of that. These streets are rough. J was taking care of a lot of bitches and his mom. Everybody always had their hand out and he didn't know how to say no."

"You expect me to believe that?" I didn't know if he was telling the truth or not. I didn't trust anything he said, but I didn't want to believe that he would harm me, not with his baby inside of me.

"Yo, Emmet started acting funny. I started thinking maybe he knew more. It's wasn't a secret that I met J to pick up some shit. J didn't want anyone to know about the case. I heard that he was thinking about snitching, but I don't know. The shit came back suicide; I didn't understand why you people wanted to know more. You don't want to believe that he killed himself!" Hassan looked at me as if I was the jury and he was a lawyer closing his argument.

I guess it was hard for some people to believe that Jerri committed suicide, but I was not moved by his story. A part of me thought he knew more. Hassan had already set me up once. How could I believe anything from him? Anyway, I was not here about Jerri. I was here about me. Jerri was gone and nothing would change that.

"What do you want from me? Why did you and that bitch set me up? You think I don't know you gave Shitara my address? Y'all sent me to jail." He had the stupidest look on his face. I could tell he was trying to think of an answer, but it seemed that he was only just realizing that he was trapped.

"Neshela, I love you!" There was nothing else he could say.

"It wasn't supposed to go that way, Shela I swear." He was stumbling over his words. I just stared at him and waited to hear more. I wanted to know the truth.

"Shitara found out that Jerri had over $600,000 in insurance. For whatever reason, she didn't believe that you were the beneficiary of the big policy. Shitara just wanted the case to be changed to murder so that she could collect the money. She planned the whole thing. I was supposed to befriend you and get as much information about you as possible, but at some point I started feeling you; it's just something about you. I let my emotions get in the way. My focus changed from getting you to protecting you, and I tried to ignore my feelings. But you're the perfect woman, classy with a little hood, sexy as hell, and you can cook. You're everything a man could want, and you're carrying my child. " He smiled. "I just love you and it happened by accident, Shela. What nigga you know peels potatoes?" Now I was smiling because we shared some fun times in the kitchen. "You were never supposed to go to jail. When you went to jail we were all surprised but it was too late to change anything. I knew that you would get off because they had no case against you. I'm sorry, my lady. I love you! I tried to convince Shitara not to go through with it. "

I believed him; he looked so sincere, and for the first time I watched a tear roll from his eyes. As it mingled with the blood on his face, my heart told me to untie him. He was still explaining and apologizing. Still, I had lost more than a month of my life and $20,000 in legal fees because of him. He was professing his love for me and our unborn child. It was too late. I looked directly into Hassan's green eyes and said, "I loved you too!"

I let the last tear flow from my eyes, then squeezed my eyelids shut and pointed the Glock at Hassan's head. I pulled the trigger as I screamed again, "I loved you too!" I had fallen for him, but I had to do what I had to do. I opened my eyes and watched the blood pouring from his head. I couldn't believe I had just killed Hassan. I called Rob. He was at the door within minutes to finish things up. He bashed me on the head with the butt of the gun. I fell to the floor screaming. Blood was dripping from my head. I wanted to beat Rob's ass. He only hit me once, but I felt like I was dying. He tied me up and fired the gun twice in the direction of my head. This is what he does for a living; my brother is a hit man, but I was scared as hell. He hit me with the gun one more time, and then he left us to die. At least that's how it was supposed to appear to the police. Rob's job was to make this whole thing look like a home invasion.

I had a feeling that something had gone wrong. I began to black out. I don't know how long I was out, but I woke up to a bright light flashing in my eyes. "Do you know who did this to you?" I could barely make out the paramedic's words. There was so much going on around me and my head was pounding. I didn't bother to reply; I closed my eyes and prayed for God to take this pain away. I heard a male voice telling me that I was going to be okay. He continued talking and told me that I was going to be transported to North Fulton Regional Hospital, and that's the last thing I heard.

Chapter 25

Closing the Door

"I can't change what happened in the past, so I'm closing the door"

-Neshela

My mother and Astar were standing by my bed when I woke up. My mother was thanking Jesus as if I was not supposed to be alive. She told me everything that happened. I pretended to be shocked. My mother said I had been in the hospital for two days. She said everyone had been praying for my quick recovery.

A few hours later an Alpharetta detective showed up in my room to question me about the crime scene. The detective assured me that the crime wouldn't go unsolved. He asked me a few questions. I told him that there was a knock at the door and I opened it without asking who it was because I thought it was my neighbor. I told the detective that it was a man at my door, and he hit me the minute I opened the door and when I woke up, I was in the hospital. I asked the detective where Hassan was. Before he could say anything, the doctor interrupted us and said that I needed more rest. The detective handed me a card and told me to call him if I thought of anything. When he reached the door, he asked, "Ms. Jones is there anything else that I should know?" My mother stood up and said, "If she remembers anything we will call you." He left without saying another word.

The following day the doctor ordered an ultrasound to check on the baby. Everything looked fine, just as I thought. I was looking forward to being released from the hospital. My doctor said that that I could go home in a few days. I couldn't wait. On Wednesday, January 8, 2009, I was excited to be going home. My mother and daughter left a few days ago, so I went home alone. The hospital was just a few miles from my house. I didn't have my gate card or house key, but I kept a spare key on the patio. I told the driver to let me out at the gate. I walked to my house; it was a beautiful day and the sun was shining. I got the key and I walked to the front door only to notice the yellow crime scene tape. I unlocked the door and entered my house.

A blood trail led to my bedroom. Black dust was everywhere and there was also a large pool of dried blood on the bed. My house looked like a scene from "CSI Miami" or "Law and Order." As I replayed the night in my head, all I could see was Hassan's hopeless face. I placed my hand on my stomach and apologized to our baby for the crime that I had to commit. I lay in the bed and placed my hands on his blood. I missed him. I couldn't ignore my feelings; his seed was growing inside of me. I thought of all the good times we shared. Too bad it had all been a lie.

The most painful memory that I have was killing the father of my child, but I truly had no choice. I rocked myself to sleep. I wished I could change things. I awoke at 3:00 in the morning to a knock at the door. When I reached the door no one was there. I took a bath but I couldn't stop thinking. It was like a nightmare that wouldn't end. I planned to stay awake until Liz and Lisa got here. They were flying in to help me pack. While in the hospital, I decided to take Rob's advice and move back to Miami. I couldn't raise my baby in a home that was supposed to be for me and Jerri. I needed to rest but I couldn't sleep. I was hoping this bath would help me relax.

Melissa picked Liz and Lisa up from the airport for me. They were supposed be here around 1:00. We would only have three hours to pack up my things. The moving company was scheduled to pick up everything at 4:30. Our flight was at 8:40; I was so ready to go back to Miami. Georgia had too many memories, and I just wanted to put this all behind me.

We boarded Delta flight 237 to Ft. Lauderdale. It seemed like the flight was over before it began. I was staying at Liz's house because I wasn't closing on my house for another week. My cars were being transported from Georgia. For the next few days I planned to relax. Liz made an appointment for me at the spa. I had already called my brother's girlfriend L to get my hair done because I looked a mess. I had to get myself together. But before I went to sleep, I wrote one last letter.

> *Dear Jerri,*
>
> *Thank you for all the wonderful memories. I love you so much and wish you were here by my side. I can't stop thinking about the way things used to be and how life would be if you were here. My heart is hurting Jerri, but please continue to live in my dreams. I see you all the time. I will always love you, I miss you so much. Sorry for any pain I may have caused you, but I can't change what has happened. It seems that you just walked out of my life, and I needed someone to fill your place. Everyone falls in love, Jerri. Sometimes it's wrong and sometimes it's perfect. Hassan was a mistake, a complete fuck-up on my part. That's why I had to do what I had to do. It will all get better in time. I don't want to hurt any more.*
>
> *This last year has been rough and so painful. I plan to live in '09, I plan to live again, Jerri. New Jersey Department of Justice is considering settling out of court for 1.2*

million. The lead detective on the case was suspended for three weeks. Shitara sending me to jail was a blessing at the end of the day, I guess. I should send her a thank you card. Oh, by the way, some people think that I was trying to get rich off your legacy. I died laughing when I heard that. I thought this was my life experience. Your friends in Newark never seem to amaze me! I guess friends wouldn't be the right word to use. Them fucking niggas in Newark never cease to amaze me. Them same niggas that wouldn't pay for your tombstone.

P.S. Good bye, I'll see you again one day. Although I'll be missing you, I'll find a way to get through this. Tell God I said thank you for the blessing that he keeps sending. Even in death you live on, I love you!

Your Better Half,

Neshela Jones

I wiped my tears and closed the journal. Tomorrow is a new day and I have set my past on fire. I was back in the place where my life began: Miami, Florida, the home of the swaying palm trees, ocean breezes and rays of energy from the sun. My spirit is home where it belongs.

Green Eyes

"Things never end the way you planned them"

-Neshela

Preview of Green Eyes

24 Months later...

My cell phone rang. I looked at the ID screen. It was an Atlanta number; I didn't bother to answer the call. I ignored the phone. I was in the middle of putting Seven to sleep. When I moved to Miami, I had no plans to go back to Atlanta or Newark. Life was so different. I cherished every moment with Astar and Seven. I lived in a waterfront house on Hibiscus Island near South Beach. I wrote children's books and Astar illustrated them.

I have erased the past. I only live in the now, the present, not even the future. Just the present. I wrote in my journal every day when Seven slept. My cell phone interrupted my train of thought. No one ever calls my phone between 12:30 pm and 2:00 pm. I was thinking it must be an emergency, but by the time I made it to the kitchen the phone had stopped ringing. The missed call is from the same Atlanta number but this time there was a message. I checked my voicemail. To my surprise it was Fulton Regional Hospital. The nurse said that Hassan had just awaken from his coma and that he did not remember anything, not even his name. She said that I was the only emergency contact listed in his chart, and if I could call back right away or come to the hospital.

I damn near dropped the phone. Hassan was alive! What in the hell was I going to do? Now I was regretting not answering the phone call from the detective. I would have known this two years ago. I had no idea that Hassan had been in a coma. I thought he was dead. Why hadn't anyone told me?

Coming Soon...

Death of a Legend

Corner Boy

Green Eyes

In Love with his Happiness

THE LATEST IN URBAN FICTION
TONETTA CHESTER

Six months ago, Jerri Hopkin's death was ruled a suicide. Now, the case has been re-opened and Neshela Jones is accused of her lover's murder. As Neshela tries to piece together the story of what happened, she falls under the spell of Green Eyes. A shocking betrayal by her closest friends leaves Neshela on her own. Suddenly she finds herself in stuck the middle of a web of lies, dodging accusations, wondering who she can trust, and trying to protect herself from the unknown figure who is framing her for Jerri's murder. 2nd title in the "New Jersey" series.

October 2010   **ISBN: 978-1-935714-02-6**

The 1990s: At the center of New Jersey's thrivin drug tra⊠ cking business is Green Eyes, a self-made kingpin whose fearsome empire echoes beyond the turnpike. Grabbing an opportunity to expand his empire, Green Eyes partners with a rising rival drug gang, and becomes a vital new member of their crew. After asmooth four-year run, the crew su⊠ers from internal rivalries and falls apart. With every man for himself, Green Eyes takes on a highly profitable but risky account which ends with disastrous and unpredictable results.

Summer 2011   **ISBN: 978-1-935714-01-9**

Connections may get you in the game, but street smarts keep you on top. Surrounded by the wealth, opulence, and support of a powerful family, Rob has unlimited opportunities, but he only wants one thing: the family business. Under the guidance of his cocaine-magnate uncle, Rob jumps into the game at the top, bypassing the soul-searing dues paid by street hustlers. Enjoying the fast life, Rob makes a crucial mistake, becomes the star of a 6 o'clock news police chase and ends up facing more than just attempted murder charges.

Fall 2011   **ISBN: 978-1-935714-04-0**

Sed easily secures protection from the outside to avoid another stint in prison, but internal operations aren't going so smoothly. Two of his runners get caught with 1000kg of cocaine. Tracy is prepared to exchange her life of luxury for years in an orange jumpsuit to protect the man she loves. Mark, however is not so willing. When Sed learns of Mark's plans for betrayal, he makes a few plans of his own. As collateral damage piles up, the stakes and tensions rise, leaving Sed and Mark struggling to rise above the ruins of Sed's empire.

Spring 2011   **ISBN: 978-1-935714-00-2**